Margaret G. Reid

THE STRAIT GATE

THE STRAIT GATE

By
ANNIE S. SWAN

Author of
"Mark Desborough's Vow," "The Better Part,"
etc., etc.

WRIGHT & BROWN LIMITED
1, CRANE COURT, FLEET STREET,
LONDON, E.C.4.

MADE AND PRINTED IN GREAT BRITAIN
BY WILLIAM STEVENS LTD., YORKSHIRE
PRINTING WORKS, YORK, AND LONDON

CONTENTS

CHAPTER ONE

BROTHERS

ON a dreary March evening two young men were together in the somewhat dingy sitting-room of a second-rate boarding-house in the vicinity of St. Paul's Church-yard. They were brothers, but bore no resemblance to each other. The younger was a tall, slenderly-built fellow, with a handsome, open face, lit by deep blue eyes, which had in their depths a peculiarly winning gleam. It was a face at which many looked twice, because it was such a true index to Jack Heyward's bright, happy, unselfish nature.

He was just three-and-twenty years of age, while his elder brother, who was standing looking moodily into the fire, was his senior by four years. In personal appearance, Philip Heyward was much the handsomer of the two. His figure was tall and well knit, his face clear cut and finely featured, his whole physique striking. But his was not an attractive face. The mouth was firm to hardness, the keen dark eyes had a subtle gleam, while the brows were knit above them, giving a look almost of harshness to the face. He looked considerably older than his years, and there were deep lines on the broad brow, and a curve at either corner of the firm, clean-shaven upper lip, which told of hard work and many cares. Evidently they had been discussing some matter of grave importance, for the faces of both wore an anxious, troubled look.

"Of course, I am extremely sorry for our mother, Jack," said Philip at length; "but, really, I warned her some time ago that the concern in which she had invested her means was not safe. She told me that she was quite content to leave them where our father had placed them—another instance of a woman's lack of business capacity. It was on the tip of my tongue to remind her that a clergyman's worldly penetration is not, as a rule, singularly brilliant or correct."

"The Parquena mines were not only safe, but very lucrative when father invested in them, Philip," Jack Heyward reminded his brother, somewhat quickly. He rather resented the tone in which Philip spoke of their widowed mother, and of the kind, indulgent father whose loss they had now mourned for ten years.

"Or they were supposed to be so. It is a common trick with rotten companies like the Parquena to return large dividends for a time to delude and ensnare new shareholders," said Philip Heyward, drily. "Well, to return to the bare question, what is to be done in the matter? Of course our mother can no longer remain in the house at Kingsmead."

"It will break her heart to leave Fairfield," said Jack, a shadow stealing over his sunny face.

"There is no use talking in that way, Jack," said his brother, quietly. "I have thought the matter over, and I see no other way but for her to come here."

Jack Heyward glanced round the dingy, comfortless place, and shrugged his shoulders.

"Would you ask her to come *here*?" he said, with peculiar emphasis on the last word in the sentence.

"In the meantime, yes. We have been very comfortable here."

"Have we?" The ghost of a smile touched for a moment Jack Heyward's lips. "But *we* are very different from our mother, who has been accustomed to a pretty house and every comfort all her days. Why not take a nice house in the suburbs; and she could bring up all her furniture from Kingsmead and keep house for you? Of course, I must shift for myself, in the meantime. I can get plenty of private teaching, I daresay. It's a blessed thing for me that I graduate at midsummer."

"You are very good at suggesting what *I* should do, Jack," said Philip Heyward, rather gloomily. "Remember that you, and not I, have been long dependent on our mother. If you had gone into business, as I desired, instead of following out your craze for medicine, you would not be at a loss now."

"But Phil, I am not at a loss. At midsummer I shall be quite qualified to begin practice on my own account."

"I daresay, but where is the money to come from to buy the practice? If you start on a venture, the probability is that you will be an utter failure."

Jack Heyward looked a trifle crestfallen.

"I half thought you might be induced to lend me a few hundreds to buy a practice, Phil. I know you have plenty."

"Anything I have is the fruit of a self-denial and hard labour of which you would be incapable," said Philip Heyward, coldly. "I do not see that I am called upon to give it to you. You must fight your own battle, as I have done."

Jack Heyward's fair face flushed deep crimson. His brother's words were unjust and undeserved, because since he began his university course, he had been a conscientious, diligent, and painstaking student, for whom colleagues and professors alike predicted a successful future.

"I am glad to be told this in time, Phil, so that I may be prepared," he said, rising as he spoke. "Well, have you any message for our mother? I am going down to Kingsmead tonight."

"Tell her I shall come when I have time and means at my disposal, and say that I am willing to do what I can for her," said Philip Heyward. "But I hardly see that there is any call for you to spend money going to Kingsmead; you were there a fortnight ago."

"My mother will be looking for one, perhaps both of us and as you are not going, I must. In her distress it is the least her sons can do to go and see her," said Jack, warmly.

"If there were no other attraction than our mother, I doubt Kingsmead would not see you so often," said Philip, significantly.

Jack Heyward bit his lips.

He was often quarrelling with his brother, but always restrained himself, because since their school-boy days Philip had always got the mastery of him in every dispute, even when Jack himself was in the right.

"Shall I tell her you think of asking her to join us in our lodgings?" he asked, pausing at the door ere he went to pack his portmanteau.

"Tell her I *have* thought of that. See what she says."

"I will tell her, too, that it will be only until I can make a home for her," added Jack, quickly. "If I had the means I would think it a shame to offer my mother a shelter like this."

"You talk very loftily. Actions speak the truth. I would advise you not to promise too much, because you know very well that you are already pledged to make a home for Edith Lancaster, and it will take you all your time to work for yourself and her," said Philip Heyward, in his dry way. "I may not promise much, but my mother knows, I daresay, that I am a man of my word."

Altogether extinguished, Jack hastily retired.

His thoughts as he proceeded with his dressing were of a strangely mingled nature. For the moment even his strong, bright hopefulness was overshadowed, and he felt impatient with himself that he could not extend a helping hand to his mother—that, indeed, he could not relieve Philip of the charge altogether. It was not easy to understand from whom Philip Heyward had inherited his narrow, grasping nature, for neither father nor mother had made the things of this world their first consideration.

Mr. Heyward, the vicar of Kingsmead, a small and not very lucrative living in Sussex, had died in the prime of his life, leaving his wife and two young lads to fight life's battle alone. Not having anticipated so early a summons up higher, the vicar did not leave his wife amply provided for. All that was left was a small fortune he had inherited from a distant relative and which, on the advice of one of his parishioners, he had invested in the Parquena silver mines, which at that time were creating a little stir in the

commercial world. The yearly income accruing from
these shares had kept Mrs. Heyward from feeling the sting
of poverty; and by living quietly and frugally she had been
able to give Jack his university course. Immediately after
his father's death, Philip, bent upon a commercial life,
had left Kingsmead for London, when he entered the
mercantile house of Gooderich Brothers, as a junior
apprentice. He had always been a strange boy, and had
caused both father and mother many anxious thoughts.
From his earliest years he had hoarded his pence, and
would even barter his playthings and sweetmeats with his
fellows, and curiously enough, always managed to obtain
the best bargain. He had never been studious, but was a
first-class arithmetician, and wrote a singularly clear, bold,
and beautiful, which at once won the admiration
and favour of the heads of the firm to whom his applica-
tion was made. It was a frequent remark with him that he
would one day be a millionare, and that, too, before he
was past middle life. The gentle mother would listen to
these words with a sad heart, and try to point him to a
higher aim in life, greatly fearing that her first-born son
was making Mammon his god. In the employment of the
Messrs. Gooderich, Philip Heyward had steadily risen.
He was not personally a great favourite with the surviving
member of the firm; his still reserved nature, and abrupt
shortness of manner and speech, were not calculated to
attract; but as a servant he was simply invaluable. In all
matters of duty he was to be trusted absolutely, for he
would not flinch a hair's breadth from its fulfilment. He
would give his employer his rightful due, even to the
uttermost farthing; and when in course of time he was
raised to the position of acting manager, he exacted the

same from all those beneath him. As a matter of course, he was cordially disliked by the clerks and young lads under his supervision; but that mattered little to him. He was working with an end in view, to attain great wealth and a high position in the social and commercial world. Beyond that he did not as yet seek to look. Although his salary now stood at three substantial figures, he lived in the plainest and poorest lodgings, half the cost of which was paid by his mother when Jack joined him in London to attend the university.

Jack was in every respect his exact antipodes. Warm-hearted, impulsive, and generous to a fault, he won friends everywhere. As might be expected from one of his nature, he fell early in love, and was betrothed to Edith Lancaster, the eldest daughter of Squire Lancaster, of Kingsmead Manor. Although the Squire lived upon his own lands, he was not a rich man. He had inherited the estate heavily burdened, and he was a middle-aged man before he had been able to redeem it. Then he had a large family, for whose needs the revenues of Kingsmead were only sufficient. In all England there was no happier home than the Manor. The sunshine of love dwelt continually there, and it was a sight to see the Squire, stout, jolly, good-natured, and always cheerful, surrounded by his boys and girls, and to hear the ceaseless din of voices and tramp of feet which sounded through the house from early morn till night. Mrs. Lancaster was a mother indeed. Large-hearted, sweet-tempered, and sympathetic, she was one who could alike rejoice with the joyful and weep with the sad. Her children worshipped her, and every one in Kingsmead loved her. Edith was the eldest daughter, and was the counterpart of her mother, with the added charms of youth and girlish grace. She was a great help in the home, and was neither too proud nor too fine to soil her hands, if need be, in labour for her brothers and sisters. It was little wonder that Jack Heyward loved her with strong and abiding love of his true and manly heart. And now, with this long preamble, we will precede Jack to Kingsmead, if you please, on the evening of that wet and stormy March day.

Chapter Two

GLEAMS OF SUNSHINE

IN the dining-room at Fairfield House sat Mrs. Heyward at her solitary tea. She was a woman slightly past middle life, and though her face was now pale and worn, it still bore traces of the beauty which in early youth had won the heart of the vicar of Kingsmead. It was a fine face, yet there was a lack of resolution about the sweet, sad mouth which told that she was not by nature fitted to breast alone the tide of life. It wore an expression of deep anxiety and care that March evening, for she had many things to trouble her, and her heart was filled with forebodings for the future. While she was listlessly toying with a morsel of toast on her plate, and allowing her tea to grow cold in the cup, she heard a brisk footfall on the gravelled path under the window, and presently the bell rang with a tremendous peal. She sprang to her feet, and when the dear familiar tones of Jack's voice fell on her ear, she hastened out to the hall.

"Well, mother, *dear* mother, how are you?" exclaimed Jack in his cheery fashion. "I'm dripping wet, so don't come near me. What a night of rain it is! I'm famished as well. I hope you have something substantial for tea."

"I will see about it, my boy," said the now happy mother as she hastened away; for at sight of Jack all her troubles seemed to melt away: his presence was like a draught of some strengthening mountain air. And when she returned to the dining-room, with sundry substantial edibles in her hand, her face had lost its expression of weariness and care, and was brightened by a happy smile. Jack was toasting his feet on the fender now, and seemed otherwise bent on making himself comfortable.   There was a close resemblance between mother and son; it was from her Jack had inherited the frank, winning face, and speaking blue eyes.

"And how are all the good folks in Kingsmead, mother mine?" he asked, thrusting his feet into his slippers, and coming over to the table. "Is it as lively a place as it was the last time I was here?"

"It has not undergone any change in two weeks' time," answered his mother. "Had you not a letter from Edith this week?"

"Oh, yes, two of them; but she doesn't descend to the gossip of the place," he said, in his bantering way. "When did you see Edith or any of them at the Manor House?"

Edith was here to-day. She has been here every day since—since the news of my trouble came," said Mrs. Heyward, with a falter in her voice.

"I guessed as much. Ay, this Parquena affair is to be a bad job for you mother," said Jack, a little soberly.

"It is. What does Philip say about it?"

"Oh, the usual thing! Of course he foresaw it long ago," said Jack, ironically. "What a money-grubber our Phil has grown, mother! He is next-of-kin to the miser who hoards his gold in a leathern bag hidden under the mattress of his bed."

The mother sighed. She knew too well how true the words Jack had spoken.

"I suppose there is no hope of anything being saved

from the smash?" said Jack in his off-hand way. "Is everything swallowed up?"

"Everything. Squire Lancaster was here yesterday, and explained it all to me. It seems to have been an infamous swindle from the beginning. I wonder your poor father ever was persuaded to sink his money in it."

"He was too good to suspect others, mother; that is the truth," said Jack, candidly. "But there's no use mourning over it now. It can't be undone. The thing is to make the best of it."

"Yes; but it is not easy for one in my widowed position, and at my age, to lose everything, my son," said Mrs. Heyward, with quivering lip.

"Of course it isn't; but haven't you two sons whose duty and happiness it will be to make you feel your loss as little as possible.

A smile shone through the widow's tears, but she slightly shook her head.

"I should not care to be a burden on my sons, and I will *not* if I can help it," she said with firmness.

Jack rose, and pushed back his chair.

"Come, sit down at the fire, mother, and let us talk it over," he said; and drawing in his mother's easy chair he placed her in it, and then threw himself on the couch at the other side of the hearth.

"Philip seems to think you should come to London, mother. Could you live there, do you suppose?"

"I could live anywhere when necessity urges, Jack. I too have thought of that, knowing, of course, that I must give up this house. Did Philip propose any plan?"

"He talked of having you to join us in our lodgings, but I suggested that he might take a house in the suburbs, and you could bring up your furniture. He didn't seem to think that would be a good plan. But if I can convince him that it will be the cheaper way for him, he will be ready enough. I hate to say it mother, but I don't think you will be very comfortable with Philip, and it will be only until I can give you a home with me."

"And what of your prospects, my boy?" asked Mrs. Heyward, somewhat mournfully.

"Why, I must get a practice somehow, though I should have to borrow the money to buy it," said Jack, stoutly. "I mean to speak to the Squire about it to-morrow. He is always so jolly and kind and willing to help a fellow. I wouldn't do anything without first consulting him."

"You are quite right; Squire Lancaster is indeed a true friend," said Mrs. Heyward, warmly. "Had this not happened so unfortunately I would have been both able and ready to help you, my son, and I was looking forward to your settlement in life with such pleasure. God's ways are not our ways, and it is sometimes not easy to keep a firm hold of the belief that all things work together for good," she added a little sadly.

A grave and beautiful earnestness came for a moment into Jack's face. Underneath his rattling exterior there dwelt a deep and abiding reverence for all things good, a pure and unsullied faith in the love and care of a Higher Power, which would have astonished some who only knew Jack Heyward in his merrier moods.

"Somehow I can't be quite cast down about this, mother, and things always come right somehow, if we just trust and wait," he said quietly. "The way will be opened up for us all somehow, you will see."

"God bless you, my boy; you have done me good already!" said his mother. "I think I have been too much alone of late. It is not good for any one to live such a quiet life as I do."

The mother and son sat talking far into the night, and when they bade each other good night at length, the widow's heart was lighter than it had been for days.

The storm spent itself at the dawning, and the morning broke full of the beauty and sunny promise of the spring. Birds twittered on every budding bough, the gentle wind whispered shyly through the young leaves, and beyond the quiet town the wide ocean stretched, shimmering and peaceful, under the beams of the bright morning sun.

Jack was early astir, and whistled and sang by turns as he made his toilet, and these snatches were like sweetest in his mother's ears.

Immediately after breakfast he set off across the fields to the Manor, with a heart as light as air. Who could be sad on such a morning? Who could look upon the waking earth, kissed into life by the sunshine, and feel the weight of any care?

When he arrived at the Manor, Jack found Mrs. Lancaster among her flower-beds. She looked surprised, but much pleased, to see him, for, needless to say, Jack Heyward was a favourite with both old and young at Kingsmead Manor.

"I am glad you have come down this week, for your dear mother's sake, Jack," she said. "Is your brother well?"

"Yes, thanks. Is Edith at leisure, Mrs. Lancaster?"

"I think so. The children have gone to the lake, but I do not think she went with them. If you go up to the drawing-room, I will send her to you. The Squire rode into the village a little while ago, but as you came by the fields you would not meet him."

"No. I am very much obliged to him and to you all, Mrs. Lancaster, for your great kindness to my mother in this trial," said Jack, as they entered the house together.

"Hush! it was very little we could do. Mr. Lancaster is greatly concerned and highly indignant over the collapse of the company. He thinks such things should be punishable by law," smiled Mrs. Lancaster. "Well, just go upstairs, and I'll find Edith."

Jack nodded, and found his way to the familiar room, where he had spent so many happy hours. There was nothing costly or magnificent about it, yet it had a charm all its own, lent by the many pretty things which Edith's fair hands had made to adorn it. Her hyacinths on the little table in the wide oriel window were bursting into exquisite bloom, and the atmosphere was redolent with their delicious perfume. Jack stood a little while admiring them and impatiently longing for her coming. She entered so softly that she was close beside him ere he was aware of her approach. Then, without more ado, he took the slender figure in his arms, and murmured all sorts of happy nonsense in her ears, very sweet to those who listen, but not of absorbing interest to the outside world.

"I declare I think you grow prettier every day, my little woman," he said at length, with all a lover's admiring fondness. He had cause to admire his love, for she was as fair and sweet an English girl as eyes could wish to see. She was about middle height, and her figure was graceful and supple, and was shown to advantage by her neat, well-fitting morning dress. Her face was clear and delicately tinted, her mouth tender and womanly, her eyes honest and true, her whole manner and appearance frank, winning, and attractive. There was no nonsense, no affectation of any kind about Edith Lancaster; she was simply a sweet, sound, healthy-minded girl, who found the world a very pleasant place to live in because of the love which surrounded her, and because of the sunny-heartedness of her nature. She loved Jack Heyward with her whole heart, and knowing she was to be his wife some day, she was not afraid to let him see it. They were well suited to each other, and bade fair to make as happy a married pair as they had hitherto been blissfully happy lovers.

"I am very sorry for your poor mother, Jack. It is very dreadful to think she has lost all her money," said Edith, presently.

"Ay, it is a serious thing for her, and it has made a little difference to me, my darling," said Jack, a little soberly. "It may not be such plain sailing for me as I expected."

"Oh, but, Jack, you will be sure to get on. You will get a practice somehow, and when you do get one there is no fear of you," she said brightly. "Why, everybody will have you for a doctor! The very sight of you would make people well."

Jack smiled.

"I hope you may be right, my darling," he said. "But, Edith, it may be a little time before I can make the dear home which is always in my mind. You know I must first help my mother. She has done so much for me."

A tear started to Edith's eye. "Why, of course; I knew you would do all this; I would have been disappointed in you, Jack, if you had thought or said anything else. Your mother first; in the meantime, dear, I am very well content to come after."

"My darling, you make everything easy for me; and you will wait for me I know, and not only wait but help me with your bright and blessed love through any struggles I may have to meet in the future."

"Yes; and our happiness, when it comes, will be all the sweeter because of that waiting," said the bright, brave, true-hearted girl. "We are both so young, dear, we can afford to wait. You know I am not yet twenty-one. What does your brother say to all this? Will he not help a little?" she added, her voice taking a somewhat graver tone.

"I don't know what to make or what to think of Phil, Edith," said Jack; for only to his darling did he speak freely and unrestrainedly about his brother. "I have to pray for patience with him. He grows meaner every day, till there is hardly a spark of manliness left in him. Self and Mammon are the only gods he will acknowledge."

A shadow dimmed for a moment the clear depths of Edith Lancaster's eyes. To her, Philip Heyward was a strange and deep mystery. Little wonder, for he was as far removed from her sunny, generous, loving nature as day is removed from night.

"We must try and not judge him too hardly, Jack dear," she said, pitifully; "and perhaps some day a great sorrow will touch his heart and make him a better man. I cannot think that he has not a good heart hidden away somewhere, for he is your brother, dear, and your father and mother were his too."

"We will hope so. Do you know, Edith, the first thing

which would touch him would be the loss of his money. I don't believe he could actually feel any other calamity."

Edith shook her head.

"You should wonder, dear, what intense feelings these kind of people have, though they are seldom revealed," she said. "We must try and love him though he is so unlovable. We must not let him drift away altogether from all the sweeter influences of life."

"My darling, what a woman you are!" exclaimed Jack, impulsively; then their stolen moments were interrupted by someone calling to Jack from outside.

It was the Squire, who had returned from Kingsmead, and wished for a word with Jack, ere he went off to a meeting of Poor Law Guardians at Hastings.

Chapter Three

COUSINS

ON a somewhat bleak and wintry-looking afternoon early in April, two ladies were seated in the drawing-room of a commodious house in one of the best streets of that pleasant London suburb, Finsbury Park. Both were young, the one not long out of her teens, a sweet-faced, lady-like girl, such as you can see any day in an ordinary English home. She was neatly but not expensively dressed, but whatever Ethel St. John wore she invested with something of her own attractiveness and grace. She was busy with a piece of fancy wool-work, one of a pair of slippers intended for a birthday gift to her brother. Her companion was considerably older, and was singularly beautiful, with a dark, refined patrician beauty, not met with as a rule, except in the higher rank of life. Her figure was tall, and carried with queenly dignity and grace. Her face, though absolutely colourless, was exquisite in feature and contour; her eyes of a deep tender grey, capable of a thousand varying lights and shadows. Her hair, dark almost as the raven's wing, was coiled carelessly about her head, and fastened with a silver pin. Her dress was a plain robe of brown velvet, buttoned high at the throat, and closely at the wrists. A piece of antique lace served as collar and

cuffs, and her only ornament was a huge bunch of prim-
roses, which showed exquisitely against the rich yet
sombre hue of her attire. Her slim white hands were
clasped behind her head, her dainty feet were resting on
the fender stool, her lustrous eyes fixed intently on her
cousin's face. For they were only cousins these two,
though sisters in heart and love.

"Say that over again, Ethel," she said, with a somewhat
eager accent in her tones. "I want to remember these
words, and think over them when I am alone."

Ethel St. John laid down her work, and leaning a little
forward met her cousin's look with one as intent and
earnest.

"You can read them yourself any day, dear Mildred.
You will find them in the eleventh chapter of Matthew,
'Come unto Me all ye that Labour and are heavy laden,
and I will give you rest. Take My yoke upon you, and
learn of Me, for I am meek and lowly in heart, and ye
shall find rest unto your souls. For My yoke is easy, and
My burden is light.,' "

"Do you believe these words to be true, Ethel?" asked
Mildred Vere, abruptly.

"Dear Mildred, I have proved them to be true. Papa
taught me their truest meaning during the long weary
weeks of his illness. But for that neither mamma nor I
could have borne his death," said Ethel, with shining eyes.

Mildred Vere was silent, still with her hands clasped
behind her, and her eyes fixed on the dancing fire.

"How long is it since Uncle Herbert died, Ethel?" she
asked presently.

"It will be four years in October," Ethel answered, very softly, for the question recalled many sad, sweet memories, which stirred her very heart.

"Did *he* believe all these words, Ethel? Had he as absolute a faith as you in Bible truths?"

"Yes, the Bible was papa's guide in everything, Mildred."

"Uncle Herbert was a brave, intrepid soldier; none were more courageous on the field of battle," said Mildred musingly; "it cannot be all nonsense; there must be something real in it when a man like him believes it all."

"Papa often said that those who were earnest soldiers of Jesus Christ made the truest and bravest soldiers of the Queen," said Ethel, with kindling eye. "After his death, in a letter General Maynard wrote to mamma, he said that Colonel St. John's regiment was different from the rest; not only did his men equal, if not exceed their comrades in bravery, but there was a manliness, a fearless upstanding for the right which set them apart. The General attributed it to the noble Christian example and influence of their gallant and beloved colonel, whose, loss officers and men alike deplored."

"I have often felt the lack of something; I have often felt in my inmost heart that this life is not all," said Mildred. "I have watched Aunt Alice and you often, and wondered why you are so different from us, from any women I have ever met. Always when I come here I go home with a miserable, dissatisfied feeling, a weariness of heart and soul. If such rest as these words speak of is to be found, none need it more than I."

Ethel St. John rose, and kneeling in front of her cousin, folded her hands on her knees, and looked up into her face.

"Dear Mildred, nothing is easier than to find that rest. Simply cast all your care on God, and rest entirely on His love. He asks from us nothing else."

"It may be easy for you; you have always been so good, my pet," said Mildred, passing her hand caressingly over the sunny head. "From your earliest infancy every influence about you has been for good. You have never lived as I have lived, within the pale of a fashionable and miserable world. You have never had to stoop to every meanness, to try and appear other than you are; in a word, you have never been trained, as I have been, that to deceive society, to keep up appearances on nothing, is not only a necessary, but a clever and admirable thing to do."

Ethel sighed slightly, and for a moment had nothing to say. She knew too well that her cousin spoke the truth. Mrs. St. John's one brother, Sir James Vere, who had received his title for his services under Government in India, had returned to England somewhat late in life, and married a young frivolous girl, whose only recommendation was her pretty face. It was a great grief to his relatives, especially to his only sister, who, though many years younger, loved him sincerely. However, the new Lady Vere was received with kindness for her husband's sake. He was not a rich man, and his young wife hurried him into the extravagance of a house in Mayfair, where she kept an establishment far beyond his means. The result was inevitable failure and exposure, under which the old man succumbed, and left his young widow with a little daughter of seven to exist upon a miserable jointure which was all that remained from the wreck. Colonel St. John did his utmost for his brother-in-law's wife, and it was to his generous kindness she owed the annuity which ought to have sufficed for her own and her little daughter's needs. But Lady Vere was not a woman who could live in retirement. The taste for fashionable life which her brief experience of it had given was too firmly rooted to be set aside, and her whole life was to spent in devising means to continue in the vortex of society. Her daughter was sent to a boarding-school, and when she approached womanhood, and developed signs of great beauty, the heart of the vain mother rejoiced within her because in Mildred she saw a new means whereby her influence in the world of fashion could be increased, and she introduced her beautiful daughter early into society, in the hope that she would make a speedy and advantageous marriage. But the time went by, and though Mildred Vere won much admiration for her personal charms, no eligible suitor sought her hand. It was a bitter disappointment to the ambitious mother, and she did not scruple to upbraid her daughter for refusing to follow in the path she pointed out. Mildred Vere was proud and haughty in the extreme, and scorned to stoop to the petty artifices which seemed second nature to her mother. Her manner, stiff, restrained and cold, was against her, and repelled many who were attracted by her looks. None dreamed what a passionate, loving heart beat beneath that cold exterior; none guessed what tumults of yearning for nobler and better life, for all the sweet ties which blessed the lot of other women, rent the heart of Mildred Vere.

Ethel St. John was the only being to whom her inner

self was revealed; her tender fingers had unlocked the closed doors of Mildred's heart, and she had enshrined herself there in a true and earnest love. She knew Mildred's weariness of their hollow and unsatisfying mode of life, she knew how proud the spirit chafed under the humiliations which ever fall to the lot of those who are only admitted within the pale, and who are merely tolerated in the fashionable world. And Ethel, in her sweet faith and love, prayed often that a new and happier life might ere long be opened up for her cousin, where the best and truest impulses of her heart would have fullest scope.

"It is easy to be good, Ethel, in a home like this," said Mildred, with a sigh. "With a mother like Aunt Alice, and a brother like Herbert, it would be a marvel were you anything else. Oh, my dear, I envy you your home! What would I not give for a happy, peaceful life, like this?"

"Perhaps some day, dearest, God will fulfil all these unsatisfied longings," said Ethel, in her pitiful, loving voice. "If you could but get a glimpse of God's love and care for you, it would make even your present life easier to bear."

"Perhaps some day, my darling, all your prayers for me will be answered. I will think over all you have said. I will read your Bible carefully, my pet, and hope to find your comfort in its pages," said Mildred, rising somewhat hurriedly. "There is Aunt Alice and mamma; so I shall have to get my bonnet on, unless mamma means to stay to tea."

"Why, of course she will! don't imagine you are going to run away like this. I'll ring for tea at once," said

3

Ethel, and touched the bell. Just then the door opened, and the two older ladies, who had been shopping together in the city, entered the room. The contrast between them was complete and marked in every way. Mrs. St. John, in her plain but handsome widow's attire, her fair face shining in its sweet motherliness beneath the white border of her mourning bonnet, looked what she saw—a thorough gentlewoman by birth and breeding. She moved gracefully, spoke in low, yet clear and pleasant tones; her whole presence was restful alike to the eye and heart.

Her sister-in-law, Lady Emily Vere, was a tall and handsome woman, with a haughty, unattractive face and piercing dark eyes. She was richly and elaborately attired in the latest style and colour, regardless that both were rather too youthful to be becoming. She moved with a great rustling of skirts, and threw herself into a low chair, exclaiming in a shrill, hard, unmusical voice:

"Dear me, shopping is *the* most wearing out thing in existence. I can tell you, Mildred, it was much against my will I came out here again, instead of going home to Curzon Street. I am quite exhausted."

"Won't you come upstairs and take off your bonnet, Emily!" said Mrs. St. John, gently. "Then after tea you could lie down for an hour."

"Oh dear no, I don't indulge myself. Time enough for afternoon naps ten years hence; and really we must be going soon."

"I wish very much you would stay and spend the evening with us," said Mrs. St. John. "We expect Herbert's college companion and his brother to-night. I should like you to see Mr. Heyward; he is a great favourite with us."

"Heyward? is he of the South Devon branch of Heywards, a very old family?" asked Lady Vere.

"I think not; his father was the vicar of Kingsmead; he has been dead some years. His mother was a Derwent of Derwent Court. I knew her slightly many years ago when we were both girls," answered Mrs. St. John.

"What do you say to staying, Mildred? We have no engagement to-night, have we?" asked Lady Vere, turning to her daughter.

"None that I know of, mamma," answered Mildred, briefly. "Of course, I shall be only too glad to stay."

"Very well; yes, thanks—I'll go upstairs, Alice," said Lady Vere, languidly, rising and following her sister-in-law out of the room.

About seven o'clock Herbert St. John returned home, bringing with him not only Jack, but his brother Philip, whom the ladies had often heard of but had never met. Mrs. St. John had frequently asked Jack to bring him down, but Philip was not of a sociable nature, and did not care to make acquaintance with new people.

Jack was perfectly amazed at the gentlemanly ease and grace of manner which his taciturn brother displayed when ushered into the presence of so many ladies, and he was quick to note also what an impression his fine appearance made upon them. When the introductions were over, Lady Vere graciously made room for Mr. Philip Heyward on the ottoman beside her, and began to talk

to him in her usual vivacious style, making many minute
inquiries regarding his pursuits and modes of life, which
Philip very skilfully parried, and gave her small
satisfaction. While he talked with Lady Vere, he watched
with close intentness her beautiful daughter, whose
appearance interested him more than that of any woman
he had ever met.

She was distinguished-looking, and what a wife she
would make, he thought, for any man whose ambition
pointed to the high position in the social scale! Uncon-
scious of the interest with which she was being regarded,
Mildred talked somewhat languidly to her cousin Herbert,
but as the breadth of the room was between Philip
Heyward and her, he could not hear her voice.

"Mildred, will you sing us something, please?" said
Mrs. St. John, when there was little lull in the
conversation.

"I am not in a very good mood, Aunt Alice," replied
Mildred; and then Philip noted the exquisite sweetness of
her voice. "And I have not many songs on the tip of my
tongue."

She rose quietly as she spoke, moved over to the piano,
and sitting down, ran her fingers lightly over the keys. A
moment more, and the exquisitely sweet yet mournful
strains of "Too Late" held her listeners spell-bound. She
sang it with passionate fervour, as if every word had its
being in her throbbing heart. When her song was ended
no one spoke, and Lady Vere looked uncomfortable, and
a trifle annoyed.

"A doleful enough ditty, surely," she said with an

expressive shrug. "Mr. Jack, surely you have something livelier in your repertoire?"

"I should not dare to sing after that Lady Vere," answered Jack, soberly; and it was a relief when the supper-bell rang.

Immediately after supper the brothers left, and as the night was stormy, the ladies from Curzon Street were persuaded not to return to town till morning.

Lady Vere bade both a most gracious good-night, and said she would be much pleased to see them at Curzon Street, an invitation which independent Jack at once inwardly declined. He rather liked, although he could not quite understand, Mildred Vere, but her mother was his *bete noire*.

Philip shook hands with Mrs. St. John and the rest, and last of all with Mildred. As their hands met, their eyes met also.

Philip murmured something about the pleasure of meeting, to which Mildred Vere replied by a slight and rather distant bow. But her colour came again when she met his gaze, and she abruptly turned away.

"Well, have you had a pleasant evening, Phil?" asked Jack, as they trudged through the rain to the station to catch the late train.

"Not bad, considering. Who is Lady Vere, Jack?"

"Mrs. St. John's sister-in-law. Her husband was Sir James Vere, of the Indian Government; I forget his post at this moment. She is an insufferable woman."

"Why so? She seemed to me much like other women," said Philip, drily.

"Do you mean to say you distinguish no difference betwixt one woman and another? Could you look at Mildred Vere in exactly the same way as you looked at her mother?" queried Jack in astonishment.

"All women are the same to me—amusing studies for a little, but I could be very easily surfeited of their company."

"You'll change your mind some day; and I hope when you do, it will be with a vengeance," said Jack, rather savagely. "Isn't Miss Vere a glorious singer?"

"Yes if one cares for that sort of thing. She is a fine-looking woman, and I believe there will be more in her than in the majority of her sex."

"Perhaps so. I am a little afraid of her. She is full of moods and fancies," said Jack; "I should think her husband, if she ever marries, will be either a very happy or a very miserable man."

"The latter, probably," said Philip, cynically; and Jack, in disgust, changed the subject.

Chapter Four

PROSPECTS IN LIFE

THE house at Kinsgmead found neither a purchaser nor a tenant for some time; therefore, Mrs. Heyward did not join her sons in London. Her one domestic was, however, dismissed, and she took in some pupils for music and drawing. Among these were the twins from the Manor. Philip Heyward very complacently allowed his mother to do these things, and poor Jack, though inwardly indignant knew by experience how vain it would be to remonstrate, or to appeal to his brother's chivalrous honour. Philip Heyward's creed was that the man who did not work had no right to eat, and he made no exception, even in his mother's case. She was able to teach, and as long as she did not overtax herself, there was no reason why she should not do it. So the months of early summer passed uneventfully away, and in July Jack graduated with honours, and left college, followed by the good wishes of all his contemporaries. He had nothing very definite in view, but one of his companions, a manufacturer's son from a stirring midland town, had told him there was an opening in Linborough for another medical man. Without mentioning his intention to Philip, Jack took train one fine day for Linborough, to investigate the state of matters for himself. He found it a busy, bustling place, pleasantly

situated on the banks of a wide and pleasant river, which
turned the wheels of the great factories which made the
industry of the place. He dined at the county hotel, and
in the course of a friendly talk with the affable landlord
thereof, he broached the subject he had at heart. The
landlord was only too willing to talk to an interested
listener about the daily increasing prosperity and rising
importance of his native town, and gave the stranger the
fullest particulars of its social, sanitary, and municipal
affairs. By adroit questioning, Jack elicited from him the
fact that there were only two doctors in the place, one too
old and infirm to attend to his patients, and the other,
sure of his position, too independent to be so attentive as
was desirable.

"In fact, sir, it's a general wonder that no young man
has ever come to start here; it's a splendid opening for one;
but I daresay when old Doctor Grimshaw dies there'll be
a power after his place. But there's a many grumble sore
enough. They won't 'ave Doctor Halbrooke, and they
can't get Grimshaw, and so they send to Chesterly if they
can afford it, but that doesn't pay, for it's a two or three
guinea job."

Jack smiled, and said he believed it wouldn't pay, then
he changed the subject, and led his host on to talk about
other matters. He had obtained the information he
sought, and returned to town with his mind firmly made
up. Instead of going out to his lodgings, he took train for
Kingsmead, and confided all his hopes and plans to his
mother, who was more than ready to share them, and
willing to follow him. if need be, to the world's end without question or a doubt, so great was her faith in her

younger son. He found the family at the Manor also very sympathetic, and when Linborough was mentioned, Mrs. Lancaster remembered that it was the post-town and railway station for Lynnstay, the country seat of Sir Hubert Lynne, whose wife was a cousin of her own. In the event of Jack settling there, it would be no difficult task to enlist Lady Lynne's sympathies in his favour. After hearing all Jack had to tell about the place, the Squire heartily advised him to lose no time in settling down, for there was without doubt an opening in Linborough for another Doctor. Thus encouraged and strengthened in his resolve, Jack left Kingsmead next day, and went straight to Linborough in search of a house. He repaired to the county hotel, thinking rightly that its affable landlord would be the best person to ask about such a matter. The end of it was that the young doctor took a house from the landlord himself, a roomy and pleasant villa, occupying a central position in the town, and surrounded by a large garden, which would at once reconcile Mrs. Heyward to her change of abode. Jack returned to town in a hopeful yet very sober frame of mind, for he had taken a serious step in life. He reached his lodgings about five o'clock, and found Philip there, partaking of his solitary and frugal tea. The elder brother looked up questioningly, for Jack's proceedings during the last few days had considerably mystified him. But he was too proud to ask a confidence which was not freely offered.

"I didn't expect to find you here at this hour," said Jack, as he drew in his chair to the table. "Do you go back to the office again to-night?"

"Yes, I've three or four hours' work before me yet," answered Philip, grimly; "this is our busiest time."

"When do your holidays come on?"

"You ask more than I'm able to tell. I see no prospect of them yet. But it is possible I may take a run to Kingsmead to see our mother in a week or two."

"She had an offer for Fairfield yesterday, Phil," said Jack, vigorously cutting down the loaf.

"Indeed; how do you know?"

"I was there last night and stayed till this morning."

"And are you going down again to-night?"

"Yes."

"You'll come to the end of your tether some day," said the elder brother with an expressive shrug; "but about the house. Is our mother likely to accept the offer?"

"Yes; it came very opportunely, for I was just wondering what she was to do with the house when she left Kingsmead."

"Has she any immediate intention of leaving Kingsmead?" inquired Philip with some interest.

"In the course of a week or so, I believe," answered Jack, carelessly.

Philip paused, cup in hand, and stared.

"Indeed, this is very extraordinary. It is unlike our mother to take a rash step without consulting me," he said, slowly.

"Possibly she thinks as I do, that you have not earned the right to be consulted," said Jack, coolly.

Philip Heyward's face slightly reddened. "It scarcely becomes *you* to insult me on the subject, seeing you have been, and are still, a burden on our mother's slender means," he said, bitterly.

"Nevertheless, our mother has thought fit to trust me so far as to be willing to make her home with me," said Jack, calmly.

"Her home with you! Where may that be?"

"I have taken a house in Linborough, where I begin practice next Monday," said Jack.

"In Linborough! Where is that? And where did you get the money to buy the practice?" queried Philip, utterly astounded.

"I have bought no practice. It has to be made. Of my success I have not the slightest doubt; and mother and I remove to Linborough immediately. I go down to Kingsmead to make arrangements for the immediate removal of the furniture."

Philip Heyward pushed back his chair and rose. He was bitterly angry that so many important arrangements had been made without consulting him, and there was mingled with his anger a feeling of chagrin that Jack seemed not only capable but willing to stand on his own legs at last.

"So you have persuaded our mother to give up her home, and to trust herself and her future to you on the *chance* of your making a practice in this place," he said, slowly. "I hope you understand that you and she do so on your own responsibilities; that I decline to interfere now or hereafter."

"I hope I do," said Jack, still coolly, pouring out his third cup of tea. "I'm not fool enough to look to you for anything, Phil, so you needn't tremble for your precious money; much good may it do you."

"I hope you will tell our mother how thoroughly I disapprove of this step," said Philip, sternly. "If you had the sense you ought to have, you would be willing and glad to take an assistantship somewhere, where your board at least would be secured. Tell her that I am still quite willing to take her in here till I see what can be done."

"I won't tell her anything of the kind; besides, she wouldn't come. I believe she knows very well you'd grudge her food," said Jack, who was in a singularly candid mood. "Well, I'm off. We'll be glad to see you at Linborough from a Saturday till Monday, when you can spare the time—and the money," he added; and with that parting shaft, which was perhaps not the kindest memory he could have left behind, Jack left the dingy lodgings behind him for ever.

Philip Heyward, with gloomy face and frowning eyes, watched his young brother's manly figure striding down the street with something of envy in his heart. There came to him in these bitter moments a strange feeling that he had missed something in life which Jack had made his own. There was brought home to him a deep sense of his own unworthy aims, a consciousness that the idol he worshipped would one day fall broken at his feet. Self and the world were not all the interests he should have at heart. Perhaps, after all, his young brother, whom he so despised, had chosen the better part, which would never be taken away, and for which a reward awaited him. These gloomy thoughts were not new to

Philip Heyward. As there is no human heart wholly bad, so there are few human natures so hardened by avarice or self-seeking but that they have their moments of weakness, their times of deep yearning after other things. Oftentimes in the silence of the night, when Jack had slumbered peacefully by his side, had Philip Heyward tossed upon an uneasy pillow, haunted by vain regrets, encompassed by doubts and fears, torn by strange yearnings for another and a better life. But the morning light never failed to dim these night thoughts, and the business of the day to dispel them quite.

When Jack turned the corner and was lost to sight, Philip moved from the window, and clapping his hat on his head, strode away once more to his dingy office and his uninteresting work. And Jack found the speeding train too slow to keep up with his impetuous eagerness; and as town and hamlet and cosy homestead flitted past his vision, he dreamed his roseate dreams of a future, in which love was the central figure. Mrs. Heyward was somewhat anxiously expecting her son, for the issues of the day were of the utmost importance to her. Needless to say, she listened with eager and sympathetic interest to the recital of his experiences at Linborough, and expressed her satisfaction at the step he had taken.

"But you must not be too sanguine; you may have a hard struggle at first," she reminded him. "For there will be prejudices to overcome, and the medical men in the town will not be likely to befriend you."

"Never fear, mother mine, I'll get on famously," Jack assured her in his cheery fashion. "And when they see my handsome mother, who looks a Derwent every

inch of her, and when Lady Lynne's carriage stands at
our door when she comes to call, as she will be sure to do,
our social position will be assured, and that is everthing;
so good-bye. I'm off to the Manor to tell them all about
it."

Then he lightly kissed his mother's brow, and went
off whistling through the sweet summer dusk, as if there
was no such thing as care in this world. His mother
looked after him with a smile and a tear, and then turned
away with an unspoken but very earnest prayer that God
would bless her boy in the new life upon which he was
about to enter.

As Jack approached the Manor House, he saw the
Squire smoking his evening cigar on the terrace, and
enjoying a chat with his wife and daughter, who were
sitting at the open window of the dining-room. All
expressed surprise at the sight of Jack, but in a few brief
words he explained his presence, and acquainted them
with the particulars of his immediate settlement in life.

"You're a plucky fellow, Jack, upon my word," said
the Squire, heartily. "You deserve to get to the top of
the tree; and you will."

"I hope so, I'm sure," answered Jack, laughingly.
"In the meantime, the lower branches will content me
very well."

"Have you written to Lady Lynne yet, Annabel?"
the Squire asked his wife.

"Not yet; but I will do so to-morrow. I am not sure
whether they are at Lynnstay or in Scotland just now,"
answered Mrs. Lancaster. "She will be very pleased to

become acquainted with you and your dear mother, I know, Jack."

"It is very kind of you to take the trouble for us," answered Jack. "Well, I must be off; it is nearly ten. Edith, will you come out a little way with me?"

Edith ran off at once for her wraps, and while she was gone the Squire asked a number of questions about the town, its inhabitants, etc., which Jack answered to the best of his ability.

"And what does your brother think of the thing? He should have a shrewd eye for business."

"He thinks I'm mad," was Jack's brief reply. And Mrs. Lancaster was quick to note the slight shadow which clouded the sunny face, telling that he had received only discouragement from Philip.

Happily, just then Edith returned, and Jack, bidding the Squire and his wife good-night, took her on his arm, and they turned down the moonlit avenue together.

"And now, my dearest, this is a farewell to happy idleness, to all our sweet nonsense for a time," said Jack. "It must be hard work now. I must keep my face to the weather, and never once look back."

Edith was silent. Her heart was stirred, for she knew that all his self-denying labour would be for her, so that one day he might offer her a comfortable and happy home.

"I shall not be able to come so often to Kingsmead now, my dearest," he went on, his hand clasping the clinging fingers on his arm.

"Time and money will be more precious than ever.
But you will not forget me, Edith. If I know you are
thinking of me, and praying for me, I shall go about
my work with a better heart."

Still Edith did not speak; her heart was full.

"Promise me that you will write often," he pleaded.
"You can guess that I will need all the comfort you can
give to help me on in my struggle."

"Jack, surely there is no need to ask all these things,"
she said at length. "Have I ever failed you yet?"

"Never, my darling; but there is no satisfying the
heart of man," he said lightly; and then after a brief
pause, his voice took a graver tone. "I can't tell you
how solemn I feel at the prospect of beginning life on
my own account. Pray for me, my dearest, as I shall
pray daily for myself, that I may be able to live up to
the highest aims of my noble profession. I often think
that of all other men a physician should be a Christian."

"Dear Jack, with such aims and aspirations you will
not only succeed, but I believe you will be a greater
power for good in Linborough," whispered Edith. "I
can follow you in my thoughts without a doubt or a fear."

Jack was silent a moment.

"We will only be parted for a little while, my darling,"
he said at length. "I don't intend to wait very long for
my wife. I shall not be afraid to ask her to climb the
tree with me after I have got my feet firmly planted on the
first branches."

"I see you have faith in me, as I have in you," said
Edith, lifting earnest, shining eyes to his manly face.
"So absolute is my trust that whenever you ask me I

shall come, knowing that my future and myself are safe with you."

"God bless you, Edith; these words alone are sufficient to nerve a man for any effort. Well, I must send you in now, my darling, for the dews are falling, and if I do not take care of my sweetheart, how am I to take care of my wife?"

They turned towards the house once more, and retraced their steps almost in silence; and on the moon-lit terrace he took her to his heart again, and bade her a fond farewell.

Chapter Five

SETTING HIS HOUSE IN ORDER

ONE December morning when Philip Heyward went to the office he found a messenger awaiting him from his employer, desiring him to bring up the morning's correspondence to his house in Cecil Street, Strand.

"Is Mr. Gooderich worse this morning, Sam?" he asked the boy, whom he knew well enough by sight as a useful member of his employer's household.

"Yessir, I guess he 'is, 'cos he beant able to come downstairs, and he's awful cross," was Sam's reply, given with a grin peculiar to himself.

"Wait a minute then, and I'll walk back with you," said Philip, but Sam shook his head.

"Can't, 'cos I'm off to Brompton Square for the doctor," he said impressively. "I tell you he's real bad."

Philip Heyward nodded somewhat gravely, and when Sam left the place he leisurely turned to examine the letters just sent in by the morning mail. Mr. Gooderich had been at the offiice the day before, and though he had certainly looked worn and ill, did not appear to anticipate any serious illness. In about half-an-hour, Mr. Heyward locked the door of the inner room, gave some directions to the clerks in the counting-house, and stepping out into the rain and foggy air, turned his steps towards the Strand. His mind during the walk was occupied by a variety of thoughts. Mr. Christopher Gooderich was now the sole surviving member of the firm, and was moreover an aged and infirm man, upon whom a serious illness would gravely tell. If it proved to be the last illness, in all probability the business would fall into the hands of Philip himself. The old man had no near relatives, certainly none engaged in commerce, and in the natural order of things would regard his confidential clerk as his successor. He had more than once hinted at it of late, and that raw December morning Philip Heyward's heart was filled with glowing visions of the future. There was nothing of sympathy or regret for his employer mingling with these thoughts, for the relation between them had never been more than that of master and servant. But they suited each other, for their natures were much akin. In other years, before Philip Heyward became connected with the firm, there had been two brothers in it, but the younger, a very different being from Christopher Gooderich, had died in his young manhood, and thus the only softening influence had passed out of Christopher's life. He sought no other partner, but plodded on his way, slowly but surely heaping up his piles of gold, hoarding it, and denying himself everything but the necessaries of life; and for what end? When the appointed hour came, could he take with him even one glittering coin? Of course Christopher Gooderich was a bachelor. A housekeeper, a grim-eyed, sour-visaged old dame, who did honour to her master's training, and the boy Sam, her nephew, were the only inmates of the house in Cecil Street. The advent of Sam had been a necessity, for

Prudence had begun to fail like her master, and was not so able as formerly for her household duties. It had been her idea that a boy would be easier to manage, and would do more work than a girl of the same age; and besides, it had been a charity to her sister, struggling to rear a family of nine on the slender wages of a bus conductor. Sam, being of a bright nature, contrived to enjoy himself even in that dingy house, and in the absence of other recreation amused himself by playing tricks on the old lady, and trying to teach a starling to speak. When Philip Heyward knocked at the door of his master's house, Prudence opened it, and her face was very grave indeed. She shook her head ominously, and in answer to Philip's inquiry said she feared her master was worse than he thought himself.

"I told him he needn't be sendin' for you to worry him with them things," she said, pointing to the packet of letters Philip took from his coat pocket ere he hung it up in the hall. "But he has his way, and must be humoured, like all his kind."

"Is he in bed?" asked Philip, as the old woman motioned him upstairs.

"Yes, and likely to be," she retorted shortly. "You know the door, second on the right; now don't you go tellin, him things to bother him, mind."

"Oh, I'll be careful enough," said Philip, and proceeded quietly upstairs. He knocked at the bedroom door, and entered without waiting for an answer. It was a bare, cheerless place, and felt bitterly cold, for the few red embers smouldering beneath a lump of coal in the grate were only a mockery of a fire. On the bed, propped up by pillows, against which his wrinkled face showed in painful contrast, lay the head of the successful firm, Gooderich Brothers. Philip Heyward visibly started to see the change a few hours had wrought upon that face. The seal of death was unmistakably set on it now.

"I am sorry to see you so ill, sir," said he with something of gentleness in his tone. Christopher Gooderich shook his head, and motioned his clerk to draw a chair near to the bed. He did so, and proceeded to open the letters he had in his hand.

"Ay, read them," said the old man languidly, but he listened with only a show of interest. Philip saw perfectly well that he was neither following nor comprehending what was being read to him, and at length stopped abruptly.

"Pardon me, sir, but I fear you are too ill to be troubled with business matters to-day," he said. "You may trust me to deal with these letters precisely as you would deal with them yourself."

"Ay, ay, put them away, I can trust you, Heyward," murmured the old man. "Put them away, and come and listen, while I say what I have to say to you."

Philip laid the letters on the bureau, and once more turned to his master.

"Hasn't the boy gone for the doctor?" he asked, bringing his restless eyes on the face of his confidential clerk.

"So he told me; probably he will be back with him

soon. Would it not be better to postpone what you have to say till he comes?" said Philip. "Possibly he may be able to give you some strengthening medicine; you seem very weak."

"Ay, I am weak; I have been slowly coming to this for a long time. He told me how it would be—a gradual declension of strength, and then a sudden collapse. I suppose a few hours or days will end it now."

Philip Heyward started.

"Oh no, sir; surely you are mistaken. That is just a morbid idea born of your weakness," he said quickly.

The old man looked keenly into Philip's face.

"No, the hand of Death, Heyward, is not to be mistaken, as you will learn some day," he said quietly. "So long as I have strength and clearness of mind, I had better say my say. You know my affairs pretty well, Heyward?"

Philip nodded.

"There are one or two things, though, which you do not know," continued the old man. "You have been my friend and confidential clerk now for seven years; I have never found you fail me; but for you the business would never have paid as it has done of late years. Although I said little I was not unobservant; you shall not go unrewarded."

Philip Heyward's heart beat, but he preserved an outward calmness of demeanour.

As you may have surmised, I have amassed a considerable fortune, the fruits of self-denial and frugal living, but I question now if that is be best way to spend one's life. It brings little enough satisfaction when a man comes to be where I am to-day. He is apt to look back regretfully, and to think it has been a poor, barren sort of life after all."

"Surely a life of hard work and self-denial can hardly be called a barren life, sir," said Philip Heyward.

"I don't know; hard work and self-denial are good things in their places, but it is by his motives that a man will be judged," said the old man.

"But there, I am wandering. Well, I have had very little to do with lawyers in my time, and of course I'm the richer by it to-day. My fortune, though large, is easily disposed of. The bulk of it is left, Philip Heyward, to you. And——"

Philip Heyward started, and an exclamation of surprise fell from his lips.

"Stay, let me finish my sentence. I ought to have said, left in trust to you," said Christopher Gooderich; "you have hitherto believed me to be without kith or kin in the world, have you not?"

"Yes, sir. I have never heard you speak of any living relatives."

"No; well, it is possible that I may have none. Let me tell you something of our family. My father was the original founder of our mercantile house, but it was a very small affair in his days, the income accruing from it not being a tithe of what it is now. But it kept his family respectably in this house. I was born here, and my younger brother Walter, and my sister Mary."

Philip Hayward fancied the old man's voice took a

deeper, more tender tone, and that his hard face seemed softened by some gleam of memory.

"Our mother died when we were all young, and our father when I was seven-and-twenty. Two years before that my sister Mary ran away from home with a singer, a worthless fellow whom my father had forbidden her to speak to. He was terribly angry, and cast her off from him for ever. He never saw her again. After his death she came in great straits to us, begging for some help. I gave her a sum of money at that time, but told her it was the first and last. It was not, however, her last appeal. Her worthless husband sent her to us again and again, but I remained inexorable. My brother Walter, however, helped her every time, and that was the cause of considerable coolness between us. It was indeed the only thing we ever quarrelled about. Walter died before he was thirty, and then I lost sight of Mary. She has one child I know, but how many more I never learned. She may be dead or alive, I cannot tell. Some time ago I got a deed made, leaving all my money to you, with the exception of a few hundreds to my housekeeper. It is in the inner drawer of the bureau, and is properly attested by two witnesses. But since I have found myself failing, I have been visited by many a strange weakness, among others a kind of remorse for my hardness of heart towards my sister. And so now I will make all the reparation I can, though it may be too late. I want you to make out a deed for me to-day

which will empower you to make every search for my
sister or her children; and after they are found, to make
over to them the bulk of my money.   For your trouble
you will receive the sum of five thousand pounds.   In
the event of all search proving unavailing, I leave my
wealth to you—you have the best right to it.   There is
some one at the door; open it.   It is Clarence."

Footsteps sounded on the stairs, and the next moment
the physician entered the room.

CHAPTER SIX

THE JOURNEY'S END

PHILIP HEYWARD rose, and turned towards the door, to receive Doctor Clarence. He was an elderly man, of genial manner and prepossessing appearance, and was, moreover, a skilful and successful physician.

"Good morning, Mr. Gooderich," he said briefly, and then glanced toward Philip.

"My manager Mr. Heyward, Dr. Clarence," said Christopher Gooderich languidly, and the two exchanged bows.

"I hope you have not been worrying yourself with business affairs, Mr. Gooderich," said the physician, approaching the bed. "I warned you long ago that you were not fit for business."

"No, no, I've not been worrying; don't go away Heyward, just go downstairs while I have a word with the doctor," said the sick man. "I shall want you again."

Philip obeyed, and found his way downstairs to the sitting room, which was unspeakably dreary and cold, for Prudence saw no reason to light the fire when her master had to be upstairs. He took up a book lying on the table and sat down at the window, but it was impossible for him to fix his attention on its pages. Although there was no traffic in the immediate thoroughfare, the

din and roar of the Strand filled the air, and from his
seat he could see the endless throng pass and repass the
entrance to Cecil Street. In about fifteen minutes the
physician entered the room for his hat and gloves,
which lay on the centre table.

"What do you think of Mr. Gooderich to-day?"
Philip asked.

The physician drew on his gloves and buttoned them
before he answered.

"I am sorry he is already beyond my aid, or any
human aid whatsoever, Mr. Heyward. But he is an old
man, and has reached the allotted span."

"He imagines he will not live many hours, Doctor
Clarence. Is he right?"

"I cannot say. It may be to-day, it may be to-morrow,
or he may linger a week. I am very sorry for the old
man. He has so few of the comforts of this life about him.
There are circumstances which can rob death of its
sharpest sting; but he is very forlorn," replied the
physician. "God morning, sir; I must go."

"Good morning," said Philip politely; and the doctor
went his way, carrying with him a vague distrust and a
somewhat unpleasant impression of Philip Heyward.

Presently Prudence looked in to say the master wanted
Mr. Heyward upstairs again, and Philip returned to the
sick-room.

"Come here, Heyward; it is as I thought. Clarence
tells me it is death," said the old man feebly. "We had
better set about getting that document written; but I've
been thinking over it, and I believe it would be better to
send for Tomlinson. We may as well have it perfectly
legal in its form. Is the boy Sam back yet?"

"I don't know, sir; shall I ring, or go and see?" asked Philip.

"Ay, by and by. Where are you? Come over here and sit down, Heyward, where I can see you," said the sick man petulantly. "Now, are you sure you understood what I said to you before?"

"Perfectly well, sir," replied Philip steadily. "You desire a search to be instituted at once for your sister Mrs.—Mrs.——"

"Rudolph Bernstein was the fellow's name. He was a German. Did I tell you he was supposed to be dead? I vaguely remember hearing that he died in poverty somewhere. There was a paragraph in a newspaper about it, I think; yes, yes, that's it. Bernstein was a notable man in his day, but he was too fond of drink."

"You desire a search to be instituted for Mrs. Rudolph Bernstein, or for her heirs," said Philip; "and when found, your fortune is to be paid over to them. Is that not right?"

"Yes; and *you* are to conduct the search—and if you succeed in finding them, you get five thousand for your share. I think you'd better send for Tomlinson, and he'll put it all right. He made out the other deed, you know, and he didn't charge much, a couple of guineas, I think, and it's always best to have things in legal form. Is the boy Sam back yet?"

Philip Heyward perceived that the frail mind was beginning to wander; and rising, he slipped downstairs, only to find that the boy was away on an errand for his aunt. She expected him back, however, in a few minutes. when he returned to the sick-room the old man's eyes were closed, and fearing to disturb even a light slumber,

Philip sat down on a chair at the door. But presently the old man opened his eyes.

"Is the boy Sam back yet?" he asked once more.

"No, sir, but he will not be long," Philip answered. "You seem drowsy; shall I draw down the blind and go downstairs? You might feel refreshed by a little sleep."

"No, no, I am not drowsy. You are quite sure you understand all about it, so that you can dictate the thing to Tomlinson when he comes?"

"Yes, sir, it is all perfectly clear to me."

"All right. Ay, ay, Heyward, this is death; and what do you suppose comes after?" he asked, fixing his eyes with singular keenness on Philip's face.

"Eternal life, sir," said Philip, gravely, uttering words which were only a sound, void of meaning to himself.

"Ay, or eternal death. I've never read much of the Bible in my time, Heyward, but I remember a verse I learned at my mother's knee when I was a child—something about a strait gate—can you remember it?"

" 'Strait is the gate and narrow is the way which leadeth unto life, and few there be that find it'," said Philip readily, for he was a regular church-goer, and was familiar with the Scriptures.

"Ay, ay, that's it, *few* there be that find it. It's quite true it's a strait gate, too strait for me to enter. I'm quite an old man, lying in the grasp of death, Philip Heyward, standing on the brink of the unknown, and I say to you that while you are still spared, seek the narrow way; never mind though you lose money by it, and you will do, for you know very well that we have not always kept in the narrow way in our business transactions. Some of them wouldn't bear the light. Give up all

these, and though you may be poorer in this life, you'll
be richer than I am to-day when you come to die.   I
wish I had my life to live over again."

"I think I hear the boy Sam back now, sir," said
Philip, anxious to change the current of the sick man's
talk.   "Shall I send him to Tomlinson's?   Where is the
office?"

"38, Chancery Lane, Tomlinson & Hodge," said the
old man.   "Ay, ay, send him off; the sooner the thing's
settled the better."

Once more Philip retired down stairs, and despatched
Sam for the solicitor, with many injunctions not to
loiter on the way.   It was now past the hour of noon, and
Philip bethought himself anxiously of the half-dozen
youths who would be idling away the precious stime
in the counting-house at St. Paul's Churchyard.

Accordingly he put on his overcoat and went upstairs
to tell Mr. Gooderich that he would return to the office
in the meantime.

"Very well.   Is the boy Sam back yet?" asked the
sick man.

"He has just gone off to Chancery Lane for the solicitor,
sir.   I shall look in as I pass, and return as soon after him
as possible."

"Very well, be sure and come back; you see you understand all about it, and I feel my mind too weak to speak
distincly to Tomlinson myself."

Philip Heyward was glad to get out of doors again.
The atmosphere of the house, the surroundings about
Christopher Gooderich, were depressing in the extreme.
Half-way along the Strand he met the boy Sam coming

leisurely along the pavement, with his hands in his pockets.

"Have you been to Chancery Lane, you young rascal?" he said severely.

"Yes, sir; and Mister Tomlinson's away from home, and so's t'other gentleman; won't be back till night," replied Sam, with a grin.

Rather dubious of the boy's statement, Philip turned off his way, and called at the office himself. It was true enough, both the principals were out of town, and would not return till evening. The clerk promised that the urgent summons of Cecil Street would be delivered to Mr. Tomlinson immediately on his return. Philip Heyward then hastily proceeded to his own office, saw that the clerks had sufficient to occupy them till closing hours, and rode back by bus to Cecil Street. It was between two and three when he arrived there for the second time. Mr. Gooderich was lying in a somewhat drowsy state, and had declined all his housekeeper's offers of nourishment. The old woman was in a state of the utmost concern, and in reply to her entreaties, Philip undertook to try and persuade the sick man to swallow some spoonfuls of arrowroot and a little wine. He succeeded, and the slight stimulant seemed to infuse some strength into the wasted frame, and he began to speak again.

"You'll wait till Tomlinson comes. I know he'll be here directly he gets the message. He's very attentive. I'd advise you, Heyward, any time you need a lawyer, to try Tomlinson. He's very moderate, and he's a shrewd fellow. Tell me what was in the letters this morning. I think I could follow you through them now."

To humour him Philip took two or three from his
pocket and began to read, but before he had finished the
old man had fallen asleep. Then Philip stole noiselessly
over to the window, and sitting in the shadow of the
curtain watched the setting sun drop like a ball of fire
into an abyss of impenetrable mist.

The gas-lamps were all lit, and the shopwindows
flaring brilliantly through the foggy air. And still the
roar of the city continued unabated. Philip marvelled
somewhat that the sick man could sleep through it all.
About four o'clock he awoke and spoke again.

"Are you there, Heyward?"

"Yes, sir," answered Philip, and in a moment was
by his side.

"Give me some more wine, I feel so sinking," he whispered with difficulty.

Philip at once held the teaspoon to his lips, but he had
scarcely strength to swallow it all. However, the few
drops revived the ebbing strength once more.

"The straight gate! *Few* there be that find it," he
repeated drowsily. "Ay, ay, *few* there be that find it."

"Perhaps you would like to see a clergyman, sir,"
said Philip Heyward. "Shall I send for one?"

A ghost of the old dry smile hovered for a moment
about the wasted lips.

"That is the last resource of a man who is afraid to
die. What could a clergyman do for me! No, no; who
said I was afraid? When so few find the straight gate
how could I?"

He turned his head again, and murmuring to himself
closed his eyes. And Philip stole back to the window,
and wished the lawyer would arrive. He feared the end

might come at any moment. He knew too well the meaning of the contracting mouth, the hollow eyes, the sharp,
drawn outline of the face, for he had seen his father die.
Another hour passed away. The fog cleared off by degrees,
and many stars shone in the wintry sky. Also above the
smoke-begrimed rooftree arose a shy young moon, the
moon which would be at its full at Christmastide. Prudence came sometimes into the room, and seeing that
her master still slept, she breathed more freely each time
as she stole away. In the kitchen Sam was crooning
a street melody to himself, interspersing it sometimes with
a word of explanation to the lame starling. Sometimes
his aunt would reprove his noise with a low "hush!"
Philip Heyward heard all those things, as he kept his
dreary vigil, and longed for the coming of the lawyer.
As the first strokes of six pealed from a hundred bells,
there was a movement at the bed, followed by a deep
groan. He hastily lit the gas, and rung the bell for
Prudence. Just as her foot was on the threshold of the
door, Philip Heyward held up his hand. She stepped
lightly to his side, and the twain watched for a moment
the brief and feeble struggle ere the spirit took its flight.
Before the echoes of the chiming bells died away, all
was over.

And, immediately the lawyer's smart double-knock
at the outer door sent an echo sounding through the
house.

Chapter Seven

TEMPTED AND FALLEN

PHILIP HEYWARD went downstairs to receive the lawyer who had already been shown into the sitting-room by Sam.

"Mr. Tomlinson, I presume?" he said courteously. "My name is Heyward, possibly you may have heard Mr. Gooderich refer to me."

"I have, frequently, sir," said the lawyer, a little thick-set man with a shrewd face and an eagle eye. "Is my client able to see me? I have come out at a great personal inconvenience, only on account of the urgent message."

"Mr. Gooderich breathed his last just as you knocked at the door, Mr. Tomlinson," said Philip, unsteadily, and his face was very pale. "I have just come from witnessing his death."

An exclamation of surprise fell from the lawyer's lips.

"Dear me, it has surely been very sudden! I saw him last week. He was never robust, of course; but was he so old a man?"

"No; sixty-eight, I believe," answered Philip Heyward. "Sudden death was the result of his malady. Doctor Clarence told me this morning that he did not expect him to live many days, possibly not over to-day."

"Indeed! Have you been with him much to-day?"

"As much as the cares of business would permit, sir," answered Philip, gravely.

"I am extremely sorry I did not see him in life," said the lawyer thoughtfully, but without any show of regret, for he had not been deeply interested in his deceased client.

"Will you come upstairs, Mr. Tomlinson?" asked Philip.

"Oh, no, thanks," answered the lawyer hastily. "Well, I shall have occasion to see you again to-morrow. Will you excuse me if I go now? I have a pressing engagement at half-past seven."

"Certainly," said Philip, readily.

"I presume you, as his colleague in business, will make all necessary arrangements? You are the nearest interested individual, seeing he has left no relatives," said the lawyer inquiringly. "Poor old fellow, he had a desolate enough life!"

"I am quite willing to do all that is necessary, Mr. Tomlinson," said Philip, quietly. Looking at his grave, unreadable face, the lawyer wondered whether he knew that his employer's death had made him heir to a great fortune, such as few men in his position could ever hope to obtain, even after a long and successful business life.

"Well, I'll be off. Can you meet me in my office to-morrow at eleven?" asked Mr. Tomlinson, drawing on his gloves.

"Say twelve," said Philip. "I am generally so much occupied in the morning, that it is almost impossible to leave my own office before noon."

From which speech the lawyer concluded that the the young man was unaware of his good fortune, and

pictured to himself the utter astonishment with which
he would receive the news.

"Very well, twelve be it. My partner and I have been
out of town to-day, arranging some settlements rendered
absolutely necessary by a birth in one of our noble
families, so you see our business connects us with both
the beginning and the end of life," said the lawyer.
"Good night, Mr. Heyward. Pray be punctual to-
morrow, if possible."

"I will endeavour to be so," answered Philip; then
the two men shook hands, and the lawyer went his way.
Philip Heyward stood where the lawyer had left him,
with one hand resting on the baize-covered table, and
his eyes fixed on an antiquated portrait on the wall.
He felt unable to move; some spell seemed to bind him
to the place, his mind seemed to be paralysed by the
force and magnitude of one idea. He heard the old
woman's slow and heavy movements in the chamber of
death overhead; Sam's restless stirring in the kitchen,
and his whisperings to the lame starling came across the
hall, and sounded in his ears; the ticking of an old-
fashioned watch on the mantelpiece helped to break
the stillness. All through life Philip Heyward remembered
with painful minuteness, every sound, every trivial detail
of these minutes. Presently he heard the housekeeper's
step on the stair, and she peered into the room. Her
eyes were wet with weeping, her hands trembling with
nervousness and emotion.

"I wish you'd come up and help me, Mr. Heyward,"
she said; "I'm not fit at my years to do all that's needed."

Philip turned towards her, and when he spoke his
voice sounded far off and strange in his own ears.

"Can't you get some woman? Have you no neighbour that would help you?" he asked harshly.

"Oh, I daresay, plenty ready enough. I'll send Sam for the Dennison's cook. She's an obliging woman, an' can hold 'er tongue," answered Prudence, in a somewhat offended tone, and hastily withdrew.

But Philip called her back.

"Look here, are you afraid to sleep in the house all night? I shall have to go and make arrangements for the the funeral and other things, and I should greatly prefer to sleep at my own lodgings."

"Afraid! no; what for? Go away by all means," said the old woman saucily; for she had taken a strange aversion to Philip Heyward, and thought he was too meddlesome in the house.

"All right—good night. I'll come to-morrow and tell you what arrangements I have made. Can you tell me where your late master's relatives are buried?"

"Yes, in Highbury Park, all of them except Miss Mary, and God only knows where *she* lies," said the old woman, wiping her eyes. "And she was the flower of the flock."

"Well, good night," said Philip, abruptly, and passing out into the hall put on his overcoat and strode out into the night. The air was bitterly cold, and away in the northern horizon there was a black cloud slowly spreading over the sky, which betokened the first snow of the season. But right overhead the stars were shining still, the moon beaming radiantly in its dome of cloudless blue. He was glad of the cold north wind to play upon his brow, which was hot and fevered, and he walked with hurried, restless steps, as if pursued by some evil thought. The tide of life still flowed uninterruptedly in the busy Strand; shop windows, gaily decorated for the festive season, had each their little knot of admirers; bus and handsom cab rattled noisily over the causeway; vendors of street wares vigorously and vociferously plied their trade, as if their harvest time had come and they dared not idle away the time. As Philip passed the entrance to the Strand Theatre, the door of a neat brougham just drawn up at the kerbstone, was opened, and two ladies alighted. The first passed unheeded, but he caught a glimpse of the face of the second and younger; and his heart beat a little faster in his breast. That queenly grace of mien, that proudly-carried head, that sweet but haughty face, could belong to none other than Mildred Vere. He stood a little aside and watched her till she followed her mother up the staircase to the private boxes, then he proceeded again on his way. At the entrance to the Temple he paused a moment irresolute, and then turned into the sweet and quiet retreat, where every sound of his own footsteps sent back an echo through the stillness. He walked restlessly up and down for a little, and then sitting down near the fountain, leaned his arms on his knees, and covered his face with his hands. Great beads of perspiration stood out upon his brow; the outcome of keen mental anguish. It was a crisis in Philip Heyward's life—that momentous hour which occurs only in the lives of some, when the good angel and the bad do fierce battle for the mastery in conscience and heart. It was a terrible conflict, such as angels look upon and tremble. An hour passed away. The cloud mounting steadily over the sky, obscured the gentle moon, and it grew dark, till the very blackness of the night fell upon the Temple gardens. The wind wailed fitfully and sadly through the gaunt naked trees, a stray snowflake hurried through the troubled air, precursor of the coming storm. When the first stroke of nine tolled sonorously from the bell of St. Paul's, the man rose heavily from his cold and dreary seat, wiped his clammy brow, and once more went his way. Was that hurried step and down-bent head, that uncertain fearful glance, the manner of a man who has won the victory, whose better self, whose nobler manhood had risen triumphant above that hour of fierce and fiery temptation? Ah, no! For the victor walks with head erect and bold triumphant steps, conscious of the approval of his conscience and his God.

Mr. Tomlinson had not to wait for the coming of Philip Heyward on the morrow. He arrived at the office in Chancery Lane punctually at the hour of noon. The junior partner of the firm, by name, Nathan Hodge, a younger and more active, though not a more shrewd man of business, was in the room with his senior, and was duly introduced to Philip Heyward. Mr. Tomlinson, glancing keenly at Heyward, fancied that in the clearer light of day he looked a much older man than he had thought him the previous evening, also that his face was lined and care-worn, as if he had fought life's battle in sore earnest.

"Well, I suppose we had better do business at once, seeing your time is about as valuable as ours," said Tomlinson, when the usual salutations were over.

"Pray find a chair, Mr. Heyward. Of course, being in my late client's confidence, you are aware that he had amassed a considerable fortune?"

"I was in Mr. Gooderich's confidence to a certain

extent, but he never told me the amount of his fortune,"
replied Philip, quietly.   "We were simply business
colleagues, nothing more."

"Ah, well, I believe my late client was not the kind
of man to make any violent professions of friendship,
he was of a cautious, reticent nature; but that he could
appreciate worth is evidenced by the manner in which
he had disposed of his wealth," said the lawyer.   "You
were with him some time yesterday, Mr. Heyward. Did
he give you any inkling of whom he had made his heir?"

"Yes. In the course of our conversation he mentioned
that I was his sole heir," answered Philip, steadily.   "I
ventured to remonstrate with him, for I had no claim
upon him.'

"Failing relatives, you had the best of all claims, my
dear sir," said the lawyer affably, and inwardly marvelling
at the composure displayed by the fortunate man.
"When my client laid his affairs before me, I ventured
to suggest that he might leave various legacies to
certain charities in the city, but he was not exactly that
kind of man.   He held curious views on the subjects of
religion and charity, and he had fully resolved to make
you his heir.   Acting upon his instructions, I drew
out a deed to that effect, which he signed in the
presence of witnesses in this office.   Mr. Hodge, hand
me Gooderich's deed."

Philip Heyward listened to the lawyer's reading of the
somewhat wordy document, listened without comprehending a word.   But at length, by a desperate effort,
he collected his thoughts and fixed his attention on what
the lawyer was saying.

"Fifty-three thousand pounds is all my client left,

which, less the housekeeper's legacy, and the sum to be invested for the benefit of her nephew, Samuel Greene, leaves you fifty thousand clear. Mr. Heyward, sir, allow me to congratulate you, and to express the hope that you will consider us worthy to be entrusted with the management of your affairs."

"Thanks, gentlemen," said Philip Heyward, rising to his feet. Face and voice were curiously calm, but the veins of his brow stood out like knotted cords. "I will see you again later in the day. In the meantime, good morning."

He was glad to breathe the outside air again, and yet, could its freshness sweep away the load on heart and brain? He had cast the die, and henceforth Philip Heyward would be holden indeed with the cords of his sin.

CHAPTER EIGHT

THE SHADOW OF A FEAR

"MOTHER, it is five months to-day since you came to Linborough " said Doctor Heyward, looking up from his newspaper one morning at the breakfast table. "A very short time it seems, doesn't it?"

"Yes, my son, and a very pleasant five months as well," replied Mrs. Heyward, smiling across the table at her boy. "This *was* the place for you after all."

"Of course it was; and, mother, I was looking up my books last night, and do you know, I have made over two hundred pounds since I came; not bad for a beginner, eh?" said the young doctor gleefully.

"Very good indeed, especially as your practice is increasing every day," said Mrs. Heyward in a very satisfied tone.

"I think I can afford a holiday now, mother; I believe I'll run down to Kingsmead for a couple of days during Christmas week."

"Do so, my boy, by all means. I am sure you must be wearying very much to see Edith."

"Of course I am; letters are all very well, you know, but they don't make up for the living presence; and besides, she says she has not been very well of late, so I feel anxious to see for myself what is the matter."

"Jack," said Mrs. Heyward after a little pause, "now that you are firmly established here, and likely to do well, I think you should not delay your marraige; I feel sure that if you had Edith here your practice would very considerably increase."

"And what about you, mother mine?" asked Jack, with an odd little smile.

"Jack, if I thought I was the obstacle, I would run away from you to-morrow," said Mrs. Heyward, smiling a little also, but speaking gravely. "There is no fear of me. I have a little, you know—the rent of Fairfield will keep me quietly; and there is Philip," she added vaguely.

"Yes, there's Philip, but seeing he has never even come once to see how we are getting along, I am afraid you can't depend much on him," said Jack. "I wonder how he's getting on, and what he's doing all this time. I don't know how the fellow can live such a life. It is beyond me altogether."

"I feel that I should like to see him, Jack. He has not answered my last letter, but I think I'll——"

"Why, mother, listen to this!" interrupted Jack, suddenly, for his eye, roaming carelessly down the obituary list of *The Times*, was arrested by a familiar name, and he read aloud the following brief announcement.

" 'At 7, Cecil Street, Strand, Christopher Gooderich, of Gooderich Brothers, St. Paul's Churchyard, in his sixty-eighth year.' Odd isn't it, that Phil never wrote to say his governor was ill; but perhaps it was very sudden."

"Dear me! I had no idea Mr. Gooderich was so old!" exclaimed Mrs. Heyward. "I wonder whether there will be any chance of Philip obtaining the business."

"Probably, seeing there's no one else to get it," said Jack, without much show of interest.

"He will most likely be very busy," said Mrs. Heyward. "But I think I'll go up to town next week, perhaps, when you are away. He might come down here and spend the Christmas holidays."

"I'll write to him one of these odd days and try and rouse him up. But I must be off. I've a five miles' tramp before me. I think I might venture to commission Thorpe to get me a horse now, mother. The brougham will come by and by," said Doctor Heyward, rising from the table. As was his wont, he kissed his mother before he went away, and then she stood and watched him out of sight.

Yes, these five months have sped rapidly and pleasantly for the inmates of the villa, and the young doctor was now an established favourite in Linborough. Doctor Holbrooke was forced to abandon his contempt for the young practitioner, and could not but admit that he was no mean rival. More than one of the county families had followed the example of Lady Lynne, who had not only received Doctor Heyward as a physician, but as an equal, a position to which Doctor Holbrooke had never attained, and never would attain, in Linborough, for he was not a gentleman, either by birth or nature. Another domestic had been added to the household at the villa, and the faithful Martha, rejoicing in the good fortune of those she so dearly loved, was as happy as the day is long, and even grew tolerant of the chimney stacks, which had been such an eyesore to her when she came first from the sunny shores of Sussex.

Mrs. Heyward's thoughts were so full of Philip that

morning that she sat down by and by to write to him, but she was interrupted by the rattle of carriage wheels, and presently Lady Lynne was announced. She rose and took the dainty figure in costly furs warmly to her heart; for she had learned to love very dearly the young and winsome wife of Sir Hubert Lynne.

"Oh, how cold it is this morning, and what a nice, bright fire!" exclaimed Lady Lynne, drawing near to the hearth. "Of course the doctor has gone out? Just as well; I want a talk with you, dear Mrs. Heyward."

"Are you all well at Lynnstay?" asked Mrs. Heyward, unfastening Lady Lynne's cloak with motherly hands. "And is that lazy baby of yours not making an attempt to walk yet? Fourteen months old, isn't he?"

"Fifteen. He is beginning to regard the floor with with interest, and to cautiously put one foot down," laughed the fair young mother. "I am consoled when grandmamma tells me his papa wouldn't walk a step till he was eighteen months. We have fully made up our minds to spend Christmas at Lynnstay this year."

"I am pleased to hear that; we shall miss you very much when Lynnstay is shut up."

"It is pleasant to be missed," said Lady Lynne, merrily. "I came down to see if you and the doctor will dine with us on Christmas Eve. You will probably receive a card to-morrow, but I to make very sure of you. Edith will be with us, but you must keep the secret from your son."

"Edith!" exclaimed Mrs. Heyward in surprise.

"Yes. Annabel wrote some time ago to say she had been poorly for some little time—had never got properly rid of a cold she caught picnicking with the children in September. If she is able she will come to us on Monday.

She has promised to say nothing about her visit to Doctor Heyward, so we will give him a delightful surprise."

"But he is talking of going to Kingsmead himself on Tuesday, for a couple of days."

"Then you must manage to keep him at home by fair means or foul," laughed Lady Lynne. "Tell him I have a friend whom I particularly desire him to meet, and that he can go just as well to Kingsmead on Wednesday as on Tuesday—that is, if my friend does not cause him to change his mind."

After some pleasant talk Lady Lynne took her leave, and Mrs. Heyward resumed her letter to Philip.

Jack laughed when he heard of the invitation for Christmas Eve, and said he supposed her wilful ladyship must have her way.

The days wore away and still no letter came from Philip. His mother, however, supposed that he would have so much to do with the winding up or the carrying on of the business, that he would have very little time to spare.

On Christmas Eve Doctor Heyward and his mother drove out to Lynnstay in one of the county conveyances, and Jack whispered to her, as he helped her to alight that in another year he would be driving her in his own brougham. They had come early by request, and none of the guests had yet arrived. They found Lady Lynne in the drawing-room, a lovely vision in shimmer and sheen of pearly satin, a mistress of whom Lynnstay might well be proud.

"Good evening, dear Mrs. Heyward. My husband has been out with his gun all day, and is late with his toilet," said Lady Lynne, heartily greeting them both. "Doctor

Heyward, will you please go down to the library for a few minutes? I have left something there, which I should like you to bring up."

"What kind of thing, Lady Lynne?" asked Jack, with a comical smile.

"Go and see; and do make haste or my guests will be here presently and you will be disappointed," she said, impatiently tapping his arm with her fan. Considerably mystified, Jack retired downstairs and opened the library door. There was a subdued and pleasant light in the room; a mingled effect of the red glow of the fire and the soft rays of a reading lamp on the centre table. Doctor Heyward, seeing a lady standing on the hearth with her back to the door, felt doubly mystified, and slightly embarrassed. Yet there was something oddly familiar in the graceful curves of the figure, something he ought to know in the sheen of that golden head. He took a quick step forward, and then the lady turned her head.

"Why! my darling, is it you or your ghost?" he stammered, in the greatness of his surprise, and the next moment she was clasped to his heart. For a little there was nothing said, but at length Jack raised the drooping head from its resting-place, and looked long and yearningly into the sweet dear face.

"Edith, you have been ill; it has been something more than you told me. Why, you are not the same; there is a great change!"

"No, dear; it has been nothing serious, only a cold, obstinate to leave me," she said gently. "And of late I have felt tired and lazy, quite unlike what I used to be. I was glad to accept dear Lady Lynne's invitation, in the hope that the change might do me good."

Jack was not satisfied. He drew her over to the table, and, holding her a little from him, looked at her again with all his anxious heart in his eyes. Yes, she was changed, much changed. Perhaps it was the sombre hue of the black lace dress she wore which showed the exceedingly lily-paleness of her face. A faint flush trembled on either cheek, and on the broad white brow every blue vein was distinctly visible. Her eyes has ever been wide and bright, but now they seemed unnaturally large, unnaturally bright. Also there was a darkening shadow about them which Jack's professional eye did not like to see.

"My darling, you have been, or are going to be very ill," he said, with a half-sob in his voice. "Why did you not tell me long ago? You had no right to deceive me so, Edith."

"Dearest, I did not deceive you," she said gently. "It was the truth I wrote, that I had not been so well since I caught that cold, gipsying with the children in September."

"Why do they let you do these mad things? It is time I had you to myself, Edith," he said impetuously. "I shall never know a moment's peace of mind now till you are my wife."

She smiled a little and turned her head away. It was to hide the rush of tears, the trembling lip. lest it should hurt or vex him more.

There was no enjoyment at Lynnstay that night for Doctor Heyward; and during the homeward drive he scarcely spoke a word. His mother guessed the cause of his silence, and refrained from commenting upon Edith's changed appearance. lest it should add to his anxiety.

He had a patient to see in the High Street, so Mrs. Heyward returned alone to the villa.

"Mr. Philip is here, ma'am," said Martha, when she opened the door. "He came at nine o'clock."

In much surprise Mrs. Heyward hurried into the dining-room, and Philip rose, smiling slightly at her evident consternation.

"You are surprised to see me, mother," he said quietly. "I only decided to come to-day. so there was no time to write. How are you, and where is Jack?"

"Seeing a patient," answered Mrs. Heyward, throwing aside her cloak and revealing to Philip's observant gaze her handsome evening attire   Her dress, a rich and costly black silk, with trimmings of jet and lace, became her rarely well. Never had Philip Heyward seen his mother look so imposing.

"You are looking at my dress," she said, with a little smile. "It was a gift from Jack on my birthday in October. It has been most useful, we go out so much. We have been dining at Lynnstay to-night."

"So Martha said," answered Philip. "Is Jack going to succeed after all?"

"Nobody ever had any doubt of it except yourself," laughed Mrs. Heyward. "Yes, Doctor Heyward is a person of no mean importance in town and county now, I assure you. His practice is quite established, and increasing every day."

"I am truly glad to hear it. You have a nice place here," he said, glancing critically round the pretty room. "I was quite astonished when they pointed out the house to me."

Yes, we are very comfortable.   I have not been so happy

6

since your father died, as I have been these five months
with your brother, Philip," said Mrs. Heyward, soberly,
as she drew in her chair to the fire, and prepared for
a talk.

Philip Heyward winced, and had no word to say.

"Now tell me something about yourself. Jack and I
were speaking of you to-day, and wondering what had
become of you. Now that I get a good look at you, I see
you stand in need of a holiday. You look years older
than you did in the summer. My son, why *will* you work
so hard? Why struggle for wealth at the cost of health
and every other earthly blessing?"

A slight flush rose in Philip Heyward's sallow cheek.

"I am beginning to think you were right, and that I
have made a mistake, mother; but I am glad to be able
to tell you there will be no need for me to work so hard
now."

"Why? Are you convinced at last that there are
other things in life more to be desired than money?"

"Not quite. Did neither of you observe the announe-
ment of Mr. Gooderich's death in the newspaper to-day?"

"Oh, yes. I quite forgot about it. Has he left the
business to you?"

"More than that—I am his sole heir," answered
Philip Heyward, rising abruptly to his feet. If his voice
trembled a little as he uttered these words, perhaps it
was only natural.

Mrs. Heyward held up her hands.

"Dear me, how extraordinary! Had he no relatives?"

"None. He was a bachelor. His only brother died
many years ago, and he has since lived quite alone."

"I am quite overwhelmed. Has he left a great deal of money, Philip?"

"A considerable sum. Fifty thousand pounds."

"Fifty thousand pounds to you!"

"Yes, to me."

Mrs. Heyward sat absolutely still. It did occur to her to think it a little hard that riches should be heaped upon the one, and that the other, more deserving, should have to labour early and late for his daily bread.

"I do not know whether to congratulate you or not, my son," she said at length, in tones which were almost sad. "Riches are sometimes a great blessing, sometimes the reverse. And they always bring with them many cares."

"You speak without weighing your words, mother," said Philip Heyward, impatiently. "Don't you see I shall be able to provide for you now, and to help Jack as I never could have done unless this money had been left to me?"

"Jack does not need your help now, and he is too independent to take it even if he did, after the way you treated him before. I think it right to say to you what I never allowed myself to say to him, that I think your conduct towards him has been most unbrotherly and unfeeling," said Mrs. Heyward, believing it her duty to be plain with her first-born son. "Of myself I say nothing. Perhaps, as your mother, I had a little claim upon your kind consideration; but I thank God that one of my boys remembered his father's dying charge."

Philip Heyward bit his lip, and there was a moment's painful silence. Against his will, memory took him back to a quiet summer evening, to a darkened room in

Kingsmead Vicarage, and again the earnest tones of his father's voice sounded in his ears, and he felt the solemn pressure of the feeble hands upon his head:

"May the God of Jacob go with my boys, and enable them to do their duty by their widowed mother."

Knowing too well how poorly he had fulfilled that charge, and how richly he deserved his mother's rebuke, he had not a word to say. He had expected to be received with pride and warm congratulations over his good fortune, and he was bitterly disappointed. Perhaps this was but the beginning of his punishment for his sin.

"You will continue in the business, I suppose?" said his mother presently.

"Of course; what else could or should I do?" he asked a trifle bitterly. "I had my mind made up to take a house in London, now that I can afford it, and ask you to share it with me, but——"

"I could not join you in the meantime," answered Mrs. Heyward, decidedly. "Until Jack marries, I would never for a moment think of leaving him; he shared with me all he had, and I owe him my truest gratitude and love."

Philip Heyward knit his brows. "You draw a very broad line between us, mother. It is not pleasant to be told so plainly how much dearer Jack is to you than I," he said gloomily.

Tears filled the eyes of Mrs. Heyward. "My son, even a mother's heart is only human. I *have* been sorely hurt and pained by your indifference to me; and in my distress I could not but cling to Jack. But, believe me, my heart yearns over you with a more passionate love than I feel for Jack, because it is so largely mingled with anxiety and fear."

"What for?" he asked with strange abruptness. "I am not the sort of man to go astray amid the temptations of a great city."

"Philip, there are many sins other than those of vice," said his mother solemnly. "There is the sin of selfishness, the sin of avarice, the sin of mammon-worship. It was for strength to fight these I prayed for you, my son; but at times my prayers have seemed to be of no avail."

"You use strong language, mother. If I have been selfish, it has only been that I might have more to spend by and by. If I have loved money, it has not been for itself, but for what it can obtain—for the position it can give to its possessor. I think you judge me with needless harshness."

"If so, I pray to be forgiven," said Mrs. Heyward, with a sigh. "Let me make one appeal to you, Philip, my dear boy, for you are unspeakably dear to me, because you bear your father's name, and because he loved you best."

She rose as she spoke and laid a tremulous hand on his arm.

"Since this wealth has thus strangely fallen into your hands, Philip, see that you use it aright. God will require from you an account of the uttermost farthing. Use it to make the world a brighter place than it is. There are many needy ones, many noble uses to which you can put your wealth. It will thus bring its own reward, for in blessing others you will be unspeakably blessed yourself."

She wondered to see the paleness of his face, the uneasy, troubled eye, the expression of care and pain which dwelt upon his brow—and her heart, yearning over him unspeakably, misgave her a little; perhaps she had spoken too harshly, too bitterly.

"Forgive me, my dear boy, if I have seemed too hard. It was out of my love for you I spoke, because I believed it my duty as a mother to warn you of your danger."

He turned away; he cast aside, with some impatience, the trembling, pleading hand. He hardened his heart, he knit his brows, and shut his lips firmly together.

"I am too much of a reprobate to be affected with what you say," he said bitterly. "Your utter lack of confidence in me has destroyed my confidence in myself. Of course you are right and I am wrong; only this is Christmas Eve, and I thought that in this immaculate household, if anywhere, I might look for a little of Christmas charity."

At that moment Jack's key turned in the lock; Mrs. Heyward hurriedly gathered up her wraps and went away to her own room. She would be alone for a little to collect her thoughts, to pray for her first-born, and to weep. Ay, a mother's tears are ever ready to flow; God help her when they are frozen at the fountain-head!

Philip threw himself into the chair he had lately left, and fixed his eyes gloomily on the fire.

When Jack entered, he did not even lift his head.

Chapter Nine

CHRISTMAS DAY

"PHIL, in the name of all that's wonderful, is it you?" Jack exclaimed, when he opened the dining-room door.

"Yes, it is I," Philip answered, gloomily enough, but neither rose from his chair nor held out his hand.

"Won't you shake hands with a fellow? Why, what is the matter with you, and where is mother?"

"There is nothing the matter with me. I think my mother has gone to bed. Is your work done for to-day?"

"Oh, my work is never done," said Jack, shrewd enough to guess that something unpleasant must have passed between his mother and Philip, but too wise to ask any questions. "What an odd fellow you are, Phil! You keep aloof from your relatives for an indefinite space of time, and then drop down upon them all of a sudden, like rain from the clouds."

Jack's easy rattling talk lifted the shadow from his brother's face a little, and for the first time their eyes met.

"I say, Phil, it's just about time you had a holiday, or you'll soon not need any more," said Jack, significantly. "Have you had to work extra hard since your governor aside? Was he long ill?"

"No, just a few hours; he was at the office the day

before his death; but the disease, of course, has had a hold upon him for years," answered Philip, briefly.

"Poor old chap! I hope he has left you the business, Phil; you deserve that, at least, seeing you have helped to make it what it is."

"He has left everything to me, Jack. Having no relatives alive he has made me his sole heir," replied Philip, steadily.

Jack whistled.

"That should mean something substantial. He was supposed to be rich, wasn't he?"

"He left over fifty thousand."

Again Jack whistled.

"And how much do you get?"

"Fifty thousand; the odd hundreds go to his house-keeper and her nephew," Philip anwered quite quietly, and without looking at his brother.

"Upon my word you take the thing very easily; you don't look very like a man who has just had a great fortune left him," said Jack. "And what are you going to do with it?"

"I daresay I'll find plenty of uses for it," said Philip laconically. "Can't I offer you a share?"

"I don't need it, thanks, I'm getting on famously," said Jack, soberly; and then the shadow of the dread which had taken possession of him that night crept over his sunny face.

"Why do you look so grave? What is the matter?" asked Philip.

"Oh, nothing. A little private trouble. No, no! money couldn't remove it," said Jack, hastily, for he could *not* confide to Philip his anxiety about his darling.

"Then if neither my mother nor you will take anything from me, what on earth am I to do with this money?" asked Philip, with such passionate vehemence that Jack stared.

"What did my mother say about it?"

"She reproached me for not helping you before," said Philip, bitterly. "As I said, it was not the spirit of charity I expected to find *here* at Christmas-time. How was I to know I was not just throwing money away, helping you to set up here? How could I tell you would succeed?"

"Of course, nobody could positively predict success, only you did not treat me very respectfully," said Jack, a trifle drily. "I believe you even hinted that I was acting like a madman."

Philip Heyward rose, and somewhat wearily passed his hand across his troubled brow. He had come down, yearning for the sympathy of his kindred, with a fixed resolved in his mind to ease his conscience by making them sharers with him in his wealth; but they would have none of it, and the unblessed gold was thrown back upon his hands. Well might he ask—"What am I to do with it?"

Looking at him, Jack's impulsive heart smote him. Remembering certain tender, pitiful words which had fallen from Edith's lips not many months ago, he spoke more gently to his brother. For if they severed him from the sweeter influences of life, as she had said, he might drift steadily away from all things good.

"I am tired; I think I shall go to bed," said Philip, abruptly. "Good night. I see I can get a train at twenty minutes to nine in the morning."

Before his brother could utter a word of remonstrance he had left the room. Then Jack threw himself on the sofa with an impatient sigh. Somehow, to-night, the world seemed all going wrong; he was out of sorts, and his hopefulness was quickly clouded by a prevision of coming trouble. He was worried about Edith, worried about his brother, about whom there was something peculiar, something which denoted a mind ill at ease. In the midst of these harassing thoughts he fell into a heavy sleep, from which he was awakened in the early morning by a vigorous peal at the surgery bell.

At breakfast Philip was moody and taciturn, and declined all invitations to prolong his visit to Linborough. Mrs. Heyward could make nothing of him, and Jack grew a little impatient with his peculiar vagaries of mood. Unconsciously, both felt relieved when he left the house, and yet the heart of the mother yearned unutterably over him, and she followed him with her earnest prayers.

Arrived in London, Philip Heyward wandered restlessly up and down the streets, not knowing what to make of himself, and inwardly anathematising the custom which ordained that no work should be done at Christmas-time. He felt envious of, and bitter against, the hurrying pleasure-seekers who thronged the streets; he smiled grimly to himself as the familiar Christmas greetings, over and over again repeated, fell on his ears. "A happy Christmas!" "A merry Christmas!" What did people mean by saying such words to each other? Why did they echo and re-echo in his ears as if in utter mockery of his misery? In all London that Christmas day there was no man more utterly desolate than Philip Heyward.

He was standing somewhat irresolutely at the gate of Charing Cross Station, when someone touched his arm, and the tones of Herbert St. John's voice fell on his ears.

"Hulloa, Heyward! Why are you standing there like a petrified man? Are you waiting for anyone?"

"No, I'm just loitering about," answered Philip Heyward, vaguely, and very gratefully returned the young fellow's genial handshake.

"Why, what a confession to make on Christmas Day! Don't you know what to make of yourself? Come out to Finsbury Park with me, and eat your Christmas dinner with us. My mother will be delighted. She often remarks that you must have a dull enough life of it now."

"I have, Heaven knows!" said Philip almost passionately. "You are very kind, but what right have I to be included in your family party?"

"The fact that you are Jack's brother is sufficient to ensure you a warm welcome," Herbert assured him, laughingly. Philip bit his lip, and slightly turned away. Always Jack! And the invitation was only given him on his brother's account! "Come on; say you'll come. We'll have a pleasant evening; my aunt and cousin from Curzon Street are staying with us, and there will be some other people," said Herbert, quickly. These words decided Philip Heyward, just as he was on the point of refusing.

"All right, I'll come, and many thanks. When do you go?" he asked, glancing at his attire.

"I shall go down by the half-past four train; we dine at six to-night. Can you be ready then? I have an engagement which will keep me all the afternoon."

"Yes, I'll meet you at the station at that time, and meanwhile I'll go home and dress," said Philip, and, with a nod, Herbert took himself off.

Philip Heyward turned his face towards St. Paul's once more, with something of energy in his step. In ordinary circumstances he would never have dreamed of accepting such a sudden invitation, but he was glad of anything to occupy time and thought to-night. He was careful and fastidious with his toilet, spending longer time upon it than he had ever done in his life.

It was just five o'clock when the two young men arrived at the house in Westwood Crescent. Herbert opened the door with his own key, and just at the minute Mrs. St. John stepped out of the dining-room, where she had been giving a last look at the table.

"Mother, here's Mr. Philip Heyward. I met him in town, and brought him down to dinner," said Herbert cheerily. "I suppose there's a cup and platter for him?"

"Surely, my son. Mr. Heyward, I am truly glad to see you," she said, shaking hands cordially with Philip. "I have often spoken of you, often said you might come down sometimes and see us. It must be so dull for you in the city since your brother left."

"Thank you, ma'am," said Philip a little awkwardly, "you are very kind."

"Oh, not at all. Well, will you come upstairs?" she said, smilingly. "Perhap's you will be able to amuse yourself alone for a little till we make our toilets; I believe the drawing-room will be empty."

She led the way as she spoke, and Philip followed her into the pretty room, which seemed quite familiar to him, so often had it been in his thoughts. Mrs. St. John stirred the fire into a brighter blaze and turned up the gas; then begging her unexpected guest to make himself at home and comfortable, she retired to her dressing-room. Philip Heyward walked leisurely round the room, looking at the pictures on the wall. While he was thus engaged, Lady Vere's shrill tones fell suddenly on his ears.

"Ah! Mr. Heyward, good evening. A merry Christmas to you! When I heard from my sister-in-law that you were here I made haste to come down, to relieve the stupidity of that interminable half-hour before dinner."

She sailed into the room, her purple *moire* rustling noisily behind her, the ornaments on her elaborate head-dress giving forth a jingling sound. Mechanically Philip Heyward turned to her, and took her graciously extended hand.

"And how are you? Do come and sit down beside me, and tell all about yourself," she said, coquettishly. "Dear me! you look as if you worked even harder than ever, yet surely *now* there can be no need?"

Philip Heyward looked at her inquiringly, as he took up his position on the hearth.

"Ha! ha! you would keep your little secret from us!" laughed Lady Vere. "But I assure you these things will leak out. I have a friend, a commercial gentleman, who told me just two days ago of the good fortune which has fallen you. Allow me to congratulate you, Mr. Heyward. Fortunes are not often so easily won."

"Do you think not? I am obliged to your ladyship for your interest in me," said Philip Heyward, rather stiffly.

"Dear me, what an utterly provoking man you are!" exclaimed Lady Vere. "Come now, tell me why you have never come to see us at Curzon Street. It is really not right of you to bury yourself alive as you do."

"You think not? Perhaps I will be mindful of your kind invitation one of these days," said Philip. "I trust Miss Vere is well."

"Oh yes, thanks. My daughter always enjoys the best of health. I fancy I hear her footsteps. She will be surprised to see you again. I think she does not know you have come."

The door opened again, and Mildred Vere stepped into the room. She started at sight of the strange gentleman on the hearth, and the colour rose in her fair cheek when she recognised Philip Heyward. Then she came towards him, bowed slightly, and turned aside to the table. She wore black to-night, a combination of lace and satin, finished at the throat and wrists with touches of scarlet-and-white. A glowing blossom of scarlet geranium nestled in her hair, showing to advantage against its dark richness.

When her daughter entered the room, Lady Vere
rose, and saying she had forgotten something, left them
alone. After a moment's constrained silence, Philip
Heyward crossed the room to the side of Mildred Vere.

"Will Miss Vere allow me to express my deep pleasure
at renewing my acquaintance with her?" he said
courteously.

The white hands played nervously with the petals of
the Christmas roses she was arranging in the glass. It
was quite a minute before she answered, and then she
lifted her magnificent eyes to his handsome face. At
last the faintest shadow of a smile touched the perfect
lips and she held out her hand.

"I see you are in earnest, Mr. Heyward," she said.
"I have pleasure to wish you a very happy Christmas."

CHAPTER TEN

HIS PROMISED WIFE

"MISS MILDRED, please, there is a gentleman in the drawing-room."

"Yes, Mellis; and has not mamma come back yet?"

"No, Miss Mildred; but the gentleman asked for you," said the maid, and, handing the card to the young lady, she withdrew.

A deep, rich flush overspread the face of Mildred Vere when she read the name on the card—that of Philip Heyward. Before proceeding upstairs, she walked over to an old-fashioned mirror, which surmounted the quaint library cabinet, and took a critical survey of her face and figure, and adjusted the folds of her sweeping brown dress. Then she went up to the drawing-room, and entered it without hesitating a moment.

"Dear me, Mr. Hewyard, are you sitting in the dark?" she said, with a perceptible nervousness of manner. "These stupid maids seem to have no conception of their duties unless they are being constantly reminded of them. May I trouble you to throw a little light on the gloom?"

"With your permission, I will wait a little. This fire-light is very delightful. I am glad to find you at home alone to-night, Miss Vere," said Philip Heyward, quietly, and after shaking hands with her, placed a chair on the hearth for her.

But Mildred did not take it. She stood behind it, with one slender hand leaning on its velvet rim, and there was a moment's brief uncomfortable silence.

"I am sorry my mother is out of town, Mr. Heyward," said Mildred, at length. "But I expect her home very shortly."

Philip Heyward made no reply, but stood looking keenly at the woman before him. He admired her greatly; it gave him a sense of pride and pleasure to look upon her beautiful face and queenly figure; she interested him in every way, more than any member of her sex had yet had the power to do. That was all; yet his errand to-night was to ask her to be his wife, to share his life and home, to give herself to him for all time. For a man in his position he was curiously calm.

"Miss Vere, I trust that my frequent visits to Curzon Street have conveyed some hint of my intentions and desires to your mind," he began slowly. "I am a plain, blunt man, who can neither use fine words nor elegant phrases, but I trust I shall make my meaning plain enough. I honour and admire you beyond any other woman; in fact, you are the only one who has ever had the power to interest me. Will you be my wife?"

Another silence ensued. Philip Heyward stood in perfect calmness, waiting for his answer.

But none came.

"My proposal cannot possibly take you by surprise, though the manner of it may," he continued, after a brief pause. "I am aware that it is the habit of men to utter extravagant language on an occasion like this. I cannot do so. But I am none the less sincere. If you will do me the honour to become my wife it shall be

7

my care that you shall never regret it. I am able to surround you with every comfort and luxury, and I will. I believe that because we are a sensible man and woman we can be happy together without expecting too much."

Mildred Vere slightly turned away her head. The magnificent eyes were strangely, pitifully shadowed; the perfect lips quivered sorely.

"I have no wish to hurry your decision. I may add that I have your mother's sanction and approval for whatever I say to you," continued Philip Heyward, with the manner and tone of a man who had studied his part for long. "Only I shall feel very grateful to you if you will not needlessly keep me in suspense."

Surely never had women been so abruptly wooed.

"Then my mother has discussed this subject with you, Mr. Heyward?" said Mildred in a strange, low voice, and without looking at him.

"I deemed it my duty to ask Lady Vere's consent before I spoke to you," Philip answered quietly. Then Mildred Vere raised her head. The look she cast upon him was one of strange, wistful pathos, of deep, sad wonder. He was asking her to be his wife, yet no word of love had ever passed his lips. Somehow that look stirred the cold heart of Philip Heyward, even as her song had stirred it a year ago at Finsbury Park. He took a step towards her, the studied expression on his face changed for one of eagerness; the wall of coldness and reserve upon which he prided himself was shaken at its foundation.

"Miss Vere—Mildred, I am in earnest, indeed I am," he said, somewhat hurriedly. "The manner of my wooing may seem strange to you, as verily I believe it is; but, believe me, I am sincere. And if I may not have you for my wife, no other woman shall ever have the chance."

She bent her head a little on her breast, the colour came and went upon her cheek; her whole attitude was answer sufficient. Strange that the passionate heart of Mildred Vere should be knit to this man in the bonds of a love which is the bane or blessing of a woman's life.

"I am waiting for my answer, Mildred," he said at length; then she moved a little towards him and gave him both her hands. He took them and raised them respectfully to his lips.

"These hands, I trust, say what your lips will not, that I may call you my promised wife?" he said inquiringly. "I thank you a thousand times. I repeat it will be my lifelong endeavour to make you happy."

Then he relinquished the clinging hands, gently placed her in a chair, and walked back to his old position on the hearth. Verily, as he had said, it was strange wooing indeed, not the wooing which can satisfy a woman's loving, passionate heart.

"Lady Vere thinks with me, that the marriage, if it is to take place, need not be delayed," he continued, after a brief pause. "At an early date I shall lay before you a statement of my affairs. I have already satisfied Lady Vere that I can give you a home not unworthy of you."

Mildred sat perfectly still. Of what interest were such details to her? Willingly would she have shared poverty, if need be, with Philip Heyward, and a word of love from his lips would have satisfied her more completely than any statement of his affairs. But the man was too blind to see it yet; so he continued in the same calm, passionless voice:

"I have not hitherto cared much for society or for making any display before the world; but of course things will be changed now. It will be my duty to see that you miss nothing in the new life to which you have been accustomed in the old."

Mildred rose with a strange, swift gesture, and extended her hand. "If you will excuse me, to-night," she said hurriedly, "I am a little upset, perhaps naturally, perhaps foolishly. We can discuss these things, if they must be discussed, another time. Will you let me bid you good night just now?"

"Most assuredly," he said courteously. "I sincerely trust I have not needlessly distressed or annoyed you. I would not do so for worlds."

"No, no! I believe—I know—you would not," she said, more hurriedly still. "Perhaps after a little you will understand better the needs of a woman's heart. Good night—good night!"

She left the room very hastily, as if in fear of breaking down.

Philip Heyward stood still for a few minutes; then something like a sigh of relief escaped his lips.

"She did not exhibit that repose of manner I expected," he said. "I am very glad it is over. The rest will be easy enough."

He leisurely left the room, walked downstairs, put on his overcoat and hat, and let himself out by the front door.

And Mildred? In her own room, with a locked door between her and all intruders, the strange commingling of emotions in her heart found relief in tears.

Shortly after Mr. Heyward left the house, Lady Vere

returned home. She heard from her maid that a gentleman had called, and that immediately after his departure, Miss Mildred had gone to her own room.

Thither Lady Vere at once bent her steps, but found the door locked against her.

"Let me in, Mildred," she said imperatively; but there was no answer. "Open the door, Mildred, or I shall be very angry," she repeated impatiently. Then there was a slight movement within, and the key was turned in the lock. Lady Vere at once entered the room. Her daughter was standing on the hearth, with one arm leaning on the mantel, and her face bent upon it.

"What is the matter with you, Mildred?" And why do you lock yourself into your room like the heroine of some absurd story?" asked her mother, coming closer, and trying to get a glimpse of her face.

"I wanted to be alone for a little while, mamma; surely there could be nothing absurd in that," said Mildred in a low tone.

"Perhaps not. Your cousins are both away, Mildred," said Lady Vere. "Mellis tells me you had a visitor to-night. May I ask who it was?"

Then Mildred lifted her head, and fixed her eyes, still wet with tears, on her mother's face.

"You knew Mr. Heyward was coming here to-night, and for what purpose, mamma," she said quietly.

"Well, perhaps I did, but anything might have prevented him," said Lady Vere, throwing herself into a chair, and beginning to unfasten her wraps. "Yes, Mr. Heyward has behaved thoroughly like a gentleman, and has earned my respect and esteem."

Mildred was silent. Lady Vere did not know what it

was that kept her from putting a direct question to her
daughter respecting the answer she had given to Philip
Heyward. But, somehow, her lips would not frame it;
therefore she went on talking in a vague fashion.

"Yes, I must say he has behaved like a gentleman;
and yet I need not wonder at that, for he is one by birth.
The Derwents of Derwent Court, his mother's family,
are one of the oldest Essex families, and the Heywards
themselves are not to be despised. These South Devon
Heywards, with whom the Dacres intermarried, are
their connections. I was sure of it, though your Aunt
Alice said no. And Mr. Heyward himself is immensely
wealthy. and I am sure will be generous with you."

Lady Vere paused a moment, for Mildred had again
turned away. "Of course, some of our friends may turn
up their noses at Mr. Heyward's business connections,
yet they need not, for trade is not so despised in society
as it used to be. The very peers themselves dabble in
commercial speculation, and isn't the son a certain noble
duke a banker? Yes, I am sure you ought to consider
yourself a very fortunate girl, Mildred Vere, remembering
your first youth is past."

Mildred Vere's proud lip curled slightly, and she turned
her flashing eyes on her mother's vain, empty face.

"Why do you say all these things to me, mama?" she
asked quietly. "I have accepted Mr. Heyward."

"My dear, good girl! I knew you would. You have
made me very happy," exclaimed Lady Vere, considerably relieved and rising, she affectionately kissed her
daughter's cheek.

Mildred strangely shrank from that caress. Then Lady
Vere sank back into her chair again, and shed a few tears.

"Of course, it will be dreadful to part with you, my child, but I must sacrifice my own feelings," she said pathetically. "And really, it is an immeasurable relief to me to think you will be so well provided for. It is a very wearing kind of life, trying to keep up a respectable appearance on really nothing."

"I have always said so, mamma," said Mildred, shortly. "I have never ceased to urge upon you to give it up, to point out to you how much happier we should be, living within our means in some quiet country place, than struggling and striving here for what we can never attain. People only despise and laugh at us. The world is not so easily deceived as you think."

An angry flush overspread the face of Lady Vere.

"Really, Mildred, that is not a proper way in which to speak to your mother. You ought to be ashamed of yourself. I hope you will exhibit a better spirit towards your husband. I warn you, he will not be so long-suffering with you as I am," she said quickly, but Mildred made no answer.

"Really now, Mildred, what's the use of quarrelling just when we should be the best of friends? I am sure I rejoice most unselfishly in your good fortune, and I am very fond of your future husband," said Lady Vere in conciliatory tones. "I have had many long and interesting talks with him, and it was a great relief to confide all my difficulties to him. I have not had anyone to trust in since your father died."

"Mamma!" exclaimed Mildred, indignantly. "Do you mean to say you confided our monetary difficulties to Mr. Heyward?"

"And why not?" queried Lady Vere, plaintively. "He

was extremely unreserved concerning his affairs—I could not refuse to be equally so with mine. And, besides, it is truly refreshing and comforting to meet a sympathising person. I must say, Mildred, you very seldom exhibit much sympathy or consideration for me—you are a perfect block of ice. I sometimes wonder whether you have any feelings at all."

Here Lady Vere wept again, and Mildred almost groaned in the agony of her spirit. Oh! why were things so hard to bear?

"And I must say, Mildred, that the fact that, after being made acquainted with our position, Mr. Heyward remained unaltered in his desire to marry you, shows that he must really be devoted to you; though I must add that I don't know how any man could fall in love with you—you are so cold and distant, and unattractive," said Lady Vere, rather hysterically. "Really, you have quite upset me. I must go to my own room, and ring for Mellis to bring me some tea."

Mildred allowed her mother to rise and depart without seeking to detain her. She was too weary and sore at heart to have strength even to think. She threw herself into the chair her mother had lately occupied, and covered her face with her hands. Oh, for some strong arm to lean upon, for some wise and prudent counsellor to guide her in this crisis of her life! Oh, that the way could be made plain to her feet! Oh, that she could feel sure that this marriage would turn out a wise and blessed step for her! Never in her life had Mildred Vere felt so desolate, so abandoned on life's sea, like a storm-tossed barque at the mercy of wind and wave. She slept but little that night, and the morning found her a pale, heavy-eyed creature, whose face was an index to the troubled heart within. Lady Vere went out shopping in the morning, and again in the afternoon to make some calls, and to proudly communicate her daughter's engagement to several intimate friends. At four o'clock Philip Heyward walked rapidly up Curzon Street, and sought admittance at the residence of Lady Vere. He was shown up to the drawing-room, where Mildred sat alone, listless and unoccupied, save by her own troubled thoughts. A burning blush overspread her face when Philip Heyward entered the room, but it quickly faded, leaving her paler than before.

"I am grieved to see you look so ill, so unlike yourself, Mildred," he said kindly, and involuntarily a tear started in her eyes. She rose from her chair, and laid her hand on his arm to enforce what she was about to say.

"Mr. Heyward, I learned from my mother last night that you had been made aware of the difficulties in which we are placed, and I wish to say to you, that if your proposal to me last night was the outcome of pity I retract the acceptance I gave. Although I am poor, I am proud; and I would be the wife of no man who only asks me out of charity."

She spoke quickly, and with rapidly flushing face. Looking down upon her from his tall height, knowing well the effort it cost her so to speak, an expression of tenderness beautifully softened the sterner outline of Philip Heyward's face.

"Mildred, I thought I had spoken too plainly to be mistaken," he said, with great gentleness. "I cannot make any professions, or use any fine phrases, as I told you, but I do assure you it is yourself alone I seek. What you have, or have not, is of less importance to me than the dust beneath my feet. Can you not believe it?"

She lifted her magnificent eyes to his face once more. Again that pathetic wistfulness, that wonderful longing, stirred his heart.

"You do care for me a little, harsh, stern, unlovable though I am, Mildred?" he said eagerly.

"Not a little, but a great deal, Philip Heyward," she said sobbingly. "And with God's help, I will be a true and faithful wife to you!"

He put his arm about her, and drew her very closely to his side. And a strange and exquisite sense of happiness, to which both had hitherto been strangers, crept into their hearts, and made those moments passing sweet. Ah, that they could but last for ever!

CHAPTER ELEVEN

SWEET SYMPATHY

PHILIP HEYWARD, now the sole head of the firm
of Gooderich Brothers, was a busier man than he had
ever been when he was only the managing clerk. He was
to be found in his private room in the premises at St.
Paul's Churchyard every morning punctually at nine
and very seldom left the place till five or six in the evening.
In spite of his great fortune, Philip Heyward was not the
man to eat the bread of idleness. He was busy answering
his private correspondence when his brother stepped into
his room one morning before ten o'clock, having just
come up from Kingsmead by the first train.

"How are you, Jack? I'm glad to see you," said the
elder brother cordially. "Have you just come from
Linborough? Is my mother well?"

"No, I have been at Kingsmead," Jack answered, and
the expression on his face caused Philip to make a guess
at the truth.

"I trust Miss Lancaster's health is improving," he
said kindly.

"Improving!" repeated Jack vaguely, as if not quite
comprehending the meaning of the word. "No, she is
very ill, hopelessly so. I suppose I must congratulate

you, Phil," he added, with a faint smile. "I have not seen you since you became an engaged man."

"Thanks," said Philip, briefly. "But, Jack, I am very sorry for you. Do you mean that Miss Lancaster's illness is really hopeless?"

"I said so," answered Jack. "She cannot live many weeks."

Philip held out his hand, and for the first time for years the brothers exchanged the fervent grip of sympathy and brotherly kindness.

"I see you are beginning to know a little about it, Phil," said Jack, again smiling a little; he could smile yet, poor fellow! though his heart was heavy as lead. "I say, old fellow, this is going to be terribly hard on me—in fact, I don't know how I am to weather it at all."

It was an immense relief to speak freely, and sitting down on Philip's stool he drew his hand wearily across his brow. His brother, looking on, felt his heart strangely stirred by an infinite pity. Ay, truly, Philip Heyward was beginning to know a little about it now, since his own heart had awakened to a deep enduring love.

"Jack, I wish I know what to say or do for you," he said sincerely. "Believe me, I am very sorry."

"Yes, I know you are, when you speak like that. Thank you, Phil, it does a fellow good," said Jack, lifting his head and looking at his brother with grateful eyes.

"I have a message from Edith for you. She would like very much for you to take Miss Vere down to Kingsmead to see her. She seems very anxious to look upon the face of your future wife."

Philip somewhat suddenly turned away.

"I don't know that Miss Vere would go, Jack, and I am very busy just now. I couldn't possibly spare a day."

"Not even for that, Phil?" said Jack, quickly. "I said to Edith I didn't think you would come, but surely you will have no objections to my escorting Miss Vere to Kingsmead. I have come down to engage a medical man to take my place at Lingorough, and I go back to Kingsmead, I hope, to-morrow."

"No, I have no objections, if Miss Vere herself has none," Philip made answer, a trifle stiffly. "It is a strange whim of Miss Lancaster's."

"Do you think so? To me, it seems very natural. In other circumstances, probably, they would have met often. And even if it is a whim, it would cost you very little to gratify it, and would satisfy her," said Jack, rising to his feet.

He knew very well Philip's dislike to every form of illness and death, and he would have been more than surprised had he known of the hours his brother had spent by the dying bed of the old man in Cecil Street.

"Well, I'm off. I suppose, as you are so busy, I needn't ask you to come out with me to Curzon Street?" said Jack, carelessly. "However, I know the way, and as I have met Miss Vere I shall not have the ordeal of introduction to face. Good morning."

"Good morning," Philip replied, and they parted once more. It was strange how in a moment restraint sprang up between them; there was an unexplained something which seemed to stand in the way of brotherly confidence and free intercourse; something more than mere disparity in years and disposition. When would that barrier be swept away?

Doctor Heyward was successful in obtaining a compentent and suitable gentleman to undertake his professional duties, and having satisfactorily arranged that important matter, he betook himself to the residence of Lady Vere in Curzon Street. He was fortunate in finding Mildred alone, her mother having gone to sleep off the fatigue of an assembly which she had attended the previous evening. Mildred was a little embarrassed, a little astonished also to see Doctor Heyward, whom, however, she at once recognised. Her natural tact and ease of manner came to her assistance, and she greeted him with a charming mixture of cordiality and shyness. Occupied as he was with his own sad thoughts he found time to admire anew the beauty and grace of his future sister-in-law. It seemed to him also that there was an added charm of womanliness about her, which greatly enhanced her loveliness.

"I am glad to see you, Doctor Heyward," she said, and gave him her hand with frank courtesy. "You must have many claims upon you during your rare visits to town. It was truly kind of you to remember me."

"I am come upon a special errand, Miss Vere," said Jack, as frankly; "else I fear you would not have seen me to-day. Before I state it, will you allow me to express my sincere and true pleasure in the prospect of one day receiving you as a sister?"

She bowed, and he saw tears gather in her eyes. Verily love had changed and softened the nature of this beautiful and haughty woman, thought Jack; and perhaps she

it was who was destined to change and soften Philip,
too.

"I have just come from Kingsmead, Miss Vere," said
Jack, beginning to pace up and down the room. "Probably Phil has told you that it is there *my* promised wife
has her home."

"Yes, he has told me," answered Mildred softly.
"He told me, too, that of late she has been far from
strong. May I hope that the genial weather has quite
restored her to health?"

Jack shook his head.

"Her days on earth are numbered. I have come with
a message from her to you. You will not refuse to grant
her request?"

"If it is in my power, surely not," Mildred answered,
awed a little by the intensity of anguish on the face of
the man before her.

"It is a very slight thing, but it will gratify her. She
would like to see you, the woman who is to be Philip's
wife, she said, before the end. Had she lived probably
you would have known and loved each other well,"
said Jack, and then paused a moment. "She thought
perhaps Philip might bring you down, but I saw him
this morning, and he is too busy to spare a day. Will you
allow me to escort you to Kingsmead?"

"Surely. If I can do no more than that for Miss
Lancaster, Doctor Heyward, I will at least do it with my
whole heart," said Miss Mildred Vere, with ready and
unaffected sympathy.

"Thanks, I thought you would," said Jack, gratefully.
"I am going home to Linborough to-night, to introduce

to my mother the gentleman I have secured to undertake my professional duties. After that, my place is at Kingsmead. Could you go with me to-morrow?"

"Willingly. Tell me the hour, and I shall be ready."

"It will be afternoon before I can be ready to leave town, but Mrs. Lancaster bade me say, you would be truly welcome to remain over night, or longer, at the Manor. Lady Vere, I trust, will have no scruples about it."

"Oh, no, my mother will not hinder me. Well, must you go now, Doctor Heyward?"

"Yes, it is more than time," said Jack. "Good-bye till to-morrow, Miss Vere. I cannot thank you as I would like to do for this kindness; but perhaps some day, when I have a better right, I will show you I was not ungrateful."

"Oh, hush, hush! What I have done is nothing," said Mildred hurriedly. "Need I assure you of my deep, sad sympathy?"

"No, I can read it in your face and eyes. God bless you, Mildred!" said Jack impulsively, and lifting the white hand tenderly to his lips, he hurried from the place. It was more than a mystery to him than ever how his brother had won the love of such a woman.

Beyond a shrug of the shoulders, and an expressive exclamation, Lady Vere made no demur against her daughter leaving home on the following day. Accordingly, Doctor Heyward and Mildred Vere travelled together to Kingsmead by the afternoon express. Jack had telegraphed their coming to Mrs. Lancaster, and the Squire was at the station with the dog-cart. He had a kind and hearty greeting for Miss Vere, and appeared considerably surprised at her appearance. The Squire's opinion of Philip Heyward was not very high, and he had several times expressed his conviction that any woman who married him deserved to be as miserable as she would certainly be. Mrs. Lancaster also looked with visible astonishment at the beautiful and distinguished-looking lady whom Jack lifted from the trap. She had expected a being so very different.

Her manner, though perfectly graceful and self-possessed, was a trifle timid, as if she felt the strangeness of her position. Mrs. Lancaster was unspeakably drawn to her at once, and not only shook hands very cordially, but after a second's hesitation, kissed her cheek.

"My dear, I must do it. It was so good, so very good of you to come. My daughter so hoped you would. Still, we could not have wondered had you refused."

"Dear Mrs. Lancaster, why should I have refused so little a thing?" asked Mildred, gently. "Believe me, I would do very much more than that if I could."

"Thank you; it is such sympathy which lightens our heavy sorrow," whispered the sad-hearted mother, as she led the way upstairs. "It is a great mystery why a young and bright life should be thus early quenched, a mystery for which we can find no solution here. God requires that we shall trust, and ask no questions—no easy task at times for our regellious hearts."

Mildred was silent, but Mrs. Lancaster was quick to see how her eyes filled with tears.

"Dinner will be served directly," she said, when she

showed her guest into the room prepared for her. "Can I send one of the servants to you? I keep no maid, Miss Vere."

"Oh, no, thanks. I can wait upon myself," Mildred said hastily. "And pray make no difference on my account. Treat me as one of yourselves, it will make me so much happier."

"My dear, it will not be very difficult to do that," answered Mrs. Lancaster, and stole away, relieved and glad to think that Philip Heyward's future wife was so very different from himself. The Squire was quite charmed with her, and at dinner addressed his remarks chiefly to her. Her conversation was unaffected, yet intelligent and enjoyable; listening to her, he was more and more astonished that she should be willing to throw herself away on Philip Heyward.

It was the sunset hour when Mrs. Lancaster came down to the library, and said to Mildred that Edith would like to see her now. Jack had been with her for an hour, but had now left the room. Mildred's face flushed a little when she turned to accompany Mrs. Lancaster upstairs. She was very nervous and sensitive, and feared lest she should not preserve a quiet and soothing demeanour in the sick-room. Mrs. Lancaster softly opened the door, and they entered together.

"My darling, here is Miss Vere," she said, and Mildred crossed the floor with quick, nervous step, and took her place at the side of the couch. Edith's brilliant but hollow eyes travelled over the graceful figure up to the exquisite face, which was softened just then into a wondrous tenderness. A look of utter satisfaction superseded the wondering surprise on the invalid's face, and she held out both her hands.

"Will you kiss me? We should have been sisters some day."

Mildred Vere, with a quick sob, put aside the outstretched hand, and drew the fragile form into her strong, tender, protecting arms.

There was no need for any words, for the heart of each spoke to the other in that meeting, in the language of sincerity and truth, which cannot be mistaken.

Instead of being sisters in name, in that vague uncertain "some day," they would be sisters in heart and love for the brief period during which the one would yet linger on earth. Weeping, Mrs. Lancaster stole out of the room, and left them alone together.

Chapter Twelve

AT REST

"THIS is a letter from my mother, Mrs. Lancaster," said Mildred Vere, one evening when the post-bag came in. She had now been a week at Kingsmead Manor, and had so entwined herself about the hearts of its inmates that they would not let her go. Her presence was like the very shining of the sun to that shadowed home. Not only was she invaluable in the sick-room, but none had such a happy knack of amusing the younger ones and keeping them quiet. Often Mrs. Lancaster would peep into the library, just before the children's bedtime, sure to find them with Mildred there, little Bert on her lap, and the others grouped about her knees, listening to some legend of long ago. Even tall Cyril would not have been absent from the story-telling hour for worlds. And Edith? In weakness and weariness she clung with such love an longing to Mildred, that both Jack and Mrs. Lancaster dreaded the time when she must go. It was no wonder then that the careworn mother looked up anxiously when Mildred spoke, and that her voice trembled a little when she asked the question.

"Does she say you are to come home?"

"No. She is going out of town to visit Lady Dacre at Epsom, and is quite willing for me to remain as long as I please."

"Thank God," fell involuntarily from Mrs. Lancaster's lips.

"Dear Mrs. Lancaster, have I indeed been of so much use to you?" asked Mildred, gently. The tired mother put one arm about the girl's shoulder, and drew her very close to her.

"My dear, my dear, so much that we shall never be able to repay it. No daughter could have done or been more to me than you," said Mrs. Lancaster. "You, indeed, came to us the angel unawares."

"It is a great joy to me to hear you say so. This is the first time I have done any good, or been of any use in the world, and I find it very sweet, too sweet to relinquish," said Mildred, with a sunny smile. "Now I shall run up and sit beside Edith for a little, till the children's hour. How I love those droll twins, and that wise and solemn Bertie, Mrs. Lancaster! I had no idea children could be so amusing, or teach one so much."

Mrs. Lancaster smiled too, and when Mildred left the room, she stood for a moment looking across to the summer woods, thinking with gratitude in her heart how strangely God had sent to them a help and comfort in their hour of need.

Edith had been dozing a little, but was now awake, and looked round with a smile to welcome the friend who was more than a sister to her.

"Have you had a nice sleep, dear?" Mildred asked pleasantly, adjusting the pillows with gentle and skilful hands.

"Yes, and I feel so refreshed. I was wondering if you would come up just now: I thought it too early for the children's hour."

"Yes, it is just half-past six. Shall I draw up the blind a little? Your room is rather gloomy, and you know everything ought to be bright about you," said Mildred, moving over to the western window. "There, that is better. I have had a letter from mamma to-day, Edith, and she gives me permission to stay as long as I please."

"How delightful!" exclaimed Edith. "But, dear, this is a strange sad life for you. We have no claim upon such love and service, and——"

She paused, for Mildred's pleading hand was on her lips.

"Hush! I am so selfish a being, Edith, that if I did not find it good and pleasant to be here, I should not stay," she said lightly.

Edith shook her head.

"I wish everyone were selfish in the same way as you," she said. "But, Mildred, are you not wearying to see Philip?"

"When Philip wishes to see me, dear, doubtless he will come. Till then I can wait," said Mildred quietly, but Edith easily guessed she did not wish the subject pursued.

"I had such a lovely dream while I slept, Mildred," she said after a little. "Perhaps it is because heaven is so much in my waking thoughts that it comes so vividly before me in my dreams. I saw it all so plainly—the gates of gold, the jasper sea, the white-robed throng, and I could hear the echo of the song of the redeemed."

Mildred looked at her a little fearfully. She had heard that persons dying of decline often laboured under such hallucinations, but there seemed to be no note of wandering in Edith's speech. Her eyes were serene and calm, her face even paler than its wont, and her whole manner quiet and unruffled. That week had wrought little visible

change in the appearance of the dear sufferer, but Mildred
did think that night that the outline of the face was growing more painfully sharpened, the hollow brilliance of
the eyes more painfully marked.

"Dear, do you feel yourself worse or weaker to-day?"
she asked, her firm gentle hand on the thin white fingers.

Edith smiled.

"Not worse, but weaker—yes, and at times I long to
be at rest. Will you read to me a little now, please
Mildred?"

"What shall I read?"

"Oh, you know—the last chapter of Revelation; there
are no written words on earth so sweet to me as those,
because I am coming fast to their realisation."

Mildred took the Bible from the table, opened it and
began to read: " 'And he showed me a pure river of water
of life, clear as crystal——' "

"Yes," interrupted Edith, "I saw that in my dream."

Again Mildred read on in a low quiet voice, somewhat
tremblingly, until she came to the words: "And they
shall see His face," then Edith interrupted her again.

"That was lacking in my dream, Milly. I seemed to
be looking for something I could not find. But the reality
will be different. I shall see His face."

Mildred sat very still, awestruck by the expression of
unutterable joy in Edith's eyes. Again a mighty wave of
yearning to be partaker with her in that joy stirred her
very heart.

"Oh, Edith," she said hurriedly, "tell me how I can
obtain that precious something, which makes even death
easy to bear. Before you go, leave me a little of your peace,
for which my heart is seeking."

Sad and wondering, Edith turned her eyes on the bent head and drooping figure by her side.

"Seeking, Mildred? I thought you had found it long ago. Why, my darling, I think you have it in your heart and do not know. Your life and actions, your very voice and step, seem to whisper that you are one of His own."

Mildred shook her head.

"No, no! I feel none of the joy of which I have heard you and others speak. I believe and know that I am a sinner, that all my life I have come short, have done very little for Christ, and though I am anxious to be and do better, I do not know the way."

"Dear, dear Mildred, you are in the way and do not know it. Your nature, still, reserved, and quiet, may never feel that ecstasy of joy which comes to some, and even then only at times. If you believe that Christ died for you, if you love Him, and truly try to serve Him, He asks no more. And you are safe against that day when He makes up His jewels."

Mildred sat up suddenly, and fixed wide, earnest eyes on Edith's face. In that moment of trembling hope, of half-believeing joy, her heart seemed almost to stand still.

"Edith, do you think so? Do you think that this long dissatisfaction which has possessed me, this yearning and striving after a better life, is truly its beginning?" she said in an intense voice. "Oh! if I could but be sure of it, I think I could be at rest."

"My darling, you remember that He that hath begun the good work in you is able to perfect it," said Edith, smiling a little. "And 'His grace is sufficient for you, and is able to keep you from falling.' Oh, Mildred, the Word is just brimming with precious promises for such needs as yours."

Mildred rose slowly, and, walking away over to the western window, stood looking out upon the shining sea. She was like a being who had walked blind-folded, and was thus unable to see the beauties of the way in which she was, But her eyes were opened now, and in a moment of time, a flash of thought, many, many things were made plain to her.

A low tap at the door, and the noise of someone entering the room interrupted her thoughts.

"May I come in?" said Jack's pleasant voice, subdued to gentleness, as it ever was in Edith's room. Mildred turned, and came over once more to Edith's couch. Jack saw her gentle ministering to his darling, watched the deft movements of the beautiful white hands about the pillows, and inwardly blessed her in his heart. Truly, the bond which these memories would make between Jack Heyward and Mildred Vere would be life-lasting.

"I shall go down now, dear," said Mildred very gently. "It is the children's hour."

She kissed the blue-veined brow, cast upon her a look of deep peculiar meaning, and softly stole out of the room.

"What a woman she is, Jack!" said Edith, when she was gone.

"Ay, God bless her!" Jack made answer, and was unable to say more.

"She will lead Philip into the right way, dear," said Edith, after a pause.

"Yes, if any angel influence can," said Jack. "The more I see and know her, I wonder the more that Philip should have won her."

"She loves him very dearly, Jack; only there is a little shadow on her heart about him. I see it at times creep into her eyes, when she is sitting apart. But I am not afraid for her. God will show her what to do, and in His good time give her His own reward."

Jack was silent, for once more the vision of his own desolation, so swiftly approaching, swept over him, shutting out all else. Although outwardly calm for the sake of others, there were moments when God's ways seemed dark and inscrutable to him, when he could not say, "Thy will be done"; when his whole manhood cried out in bitter rebellion, for the light and desire of his life he had to watch daily slipping from him. It would have been strange, indeed, had it been otherwise; it is not in an hour's time that humanity can reach the uppermost heights of self-abnegation; often it takes a life-long crucifixion before we can say, "Not mine, but Thine, *all* Thine."

"Jack"—very gently the clinging fingers touched his arm—"will you tell me, dear, how long you think I have still to wait with you?"

"Are you so eager to be gone from us, Edith?" he asked quickly.

"No, no, but at times this weariness, this terrible langour, makes me faint for release. I would not be selfish, my dearest, but now I think it might be better for you all if I were away."

He shook his head, not daring to trust his voice. Better for them all if she were away! So long as they had that room to enter, so long as the fragile figure and the sweet, patient face remained, they could bear the thought of separation and grudge the days passing one by one. But if the room were empty, what then?

"Tell me, Jack!" she pleaded more earnestly still.

"My darling, it is impossible to say. I have seen many weaker than you linger for weeks, yet it is possible the end may come any day."

"Any day? perhaps to-morrow?" she repeated. "It is well to be prepared. Well, dear, there is just one little thing I have to say to you, only one. You know all I feel on the subject of your work."

"Yes, what is the other thing, Edith?"

"You will not be angry with me, Jack?"

Angry! He could have smiled at the word. She laid her hand on his again, as if to enforce what she was about to say.

"It is this, and you must not wince or turn away. If in the time to come, my dearest, any other love should come to you, as I hope and pray it may, promise me you will let no memory of me stand in the way. I have always thought, and do think, that no man needs a wife more than a physician. She can so increase his usefulness, so extend his influence, so help him in every way. You will remember what I said about it, Jack, and think of it as one of my last prayers."

He almost flung her hand from him, and started to his feet.

"My darling, if you love me, spare me!" he said hoarsely. "I cannot bear much more. A wife when you are gone, any wife but you—God forbid!"

"Hush, hush, Jack! the time may come when you will remember these wild words with pain. Well, I will

never speak of it again. Don't turn away from me. I
spoke in love."

He came back to her again, but her strength was spent,
and she could say no more. That day was the last upon
which she retained perfect consciousness.

The hearts of those who loved her were torn during
the next and many succeeding days, by the wanderings
of her delirium, by paroxysms of pain, which they were
powerless to relieve. All were glad at length when the
tired eyes closed upon the earth she had loved so well,
when the gentle suffering spirit winged its way to the
city of pure gold, when the weary feet touched the
borders of the jasper sea.

Something of her sweet peace remained to hallow the
stricken ones left behind. God remembered them in their
sorrow, and sustained them with His love. The influences
of that time would never be effaced from the memories
and lives of those who shared them.

CHAPTER THIRTEEN

THE TRUST OF LOVE

"MANOR HOUSE,
"KINGSMEAD, *3rd June*, 18—.

"MY DEAR PHILIP—Just a line to tell you I am coming home to-morrow at noon, and will look for you at Curzon Street after business hours are over. It is three weeks to-day since I came to Kingsmead; it seems so much shorter than that, and yet I have learned so much in these weeks, more than I have ever done in my life. Your brother returned to Linborough yesterday, the day after the funeral. I was so sorry you did not come. I missed you, and I think Jack did. Poor fellow! my heart bleeds for him; yet he bears up so bravely. They are all wonderfully well here. Do you know, dear, I have grown to love this place and its inmates, and I think they all love me. It is with the utmost difficulty I have persuaded them to let me go at last; but I feel that I owe it to mamma and you to come back now. I can do no more here, except perhaps comfort them a little. I will tell you all the rest when I see you. I seem to have so much to say, it is so long since we had a good talk. Hoping to see you to-morrow,

"I am, affectionately yours,
MILDRED VERE."

Such was the letter which occupied Philip Heyward's thoughts one morning in his office. He sat before his writing-table with it spread before him, the yellow rays of the June sunshine falling aslant the page, shading every delicate line and curve of the beautiful handwriting. It was a quiet, kind, womanly letter, not over-burdened certainly with endearing phrases or fond expressions, but it was sincere. He knew that when she said she had missed him she meant it, and he felt glad that he could be sure of that. Slowly, yet steadily and surely love was rooting itself in the heart of Philip Heyward; already he felt this woman so dear, so necessary, to him that he was a little impatient of himself. He had not intended that this should be. His motive in seeking a wife had been a desire for a fuller existence, new interests, new cares, new duties which should not userp the place of the old, but only to fill up certain gaps in his life. The loneliness of his present life had grown intolerable to him; the monotony of his days, the dull round of duty, which was fulfilled daily and hourly with punctual rigidity, had become irksome as a task; the desire for change came upon him too strongly to be overcome. There was another reason too, and that the strongest of all, although unconfessed to himself—conscience, stern and relentless, gave him rest neither night nor day. The hours spent alone in the loveless solitude of his dingy lodging were haunted by the spectre of perpetual self-reproach.

The cry of the widow and the orphan seemed to ring continually in his ears; the gold of which he had defrauded them remained a curse upon his hands. It was of no avail to tell himself that in all probability there might be neither widow nor orphan legally entitled to Christopher Gooderich's wealth. It was a sophism with which conscience refused to be satisfied. The fact remained that he

THE TRUST OF LOVE

had betrayed the trust reposed in him by a dying man, whose last words too often rang their changes in his ears—"Strait is the gate and narrow is the way which leadeth unto life, and few there be that find it." Ay, few indeed, and Philip Heyward felt himself to be one of the "many" who throng that broader way which leadeth to destruction. There were times when he felt "almost persuaded" to make reparation for his sin, and institute the search for Mary Gooderich or her children. But again selfish cowardice stepped in, and whispered how humiliating it would be to acknowledge past misdeeds to the woman he had asked to be his wife; perhaps even she might cast him off for ever! As love for her became a deeper and more absorbing reality in his heart, fainter and fainter grew the impulse to atone.

He desired to stand well in her eyes. He had heard her express contempt for hypocrisy and self-seeking—how then could he proclaim himself to her as guilty of both? So, day by day, the way grew narrower to Philip Heyward, until the strait gate seemed closed against him for ever. He was a moody and miserable man, although the hours spent with Mildred infused some gleams of fearful joy into his heart. It was his hope that when he had built up his home, when they gathered friends under their roof-tree and about their board, the exercise of social duties would be something of an antidote to his care. Vain hope! Vain delusion! Couscience will not thus be baulked of her avenging sting. Long seemed the hours of that day to Philip Heyward; he marvelled at his own impatience, his longing for the evening to come. At the earliest possible moment he left his office and proceeded to Curzon Street. He was later than his wont,

however, for seven was pealing from the city bells when
he stood at the familiar door.

Yes, Miss Vere had returned, the servant hastened to
assure him. Would he step into the library or up to the
drawing-room, where the ladies were entertaining some
visitors?

In no mood for seeing strangers, Mr. Heyward hastily
said he would go into the library and wait till Miss Vere
was at liberty. She did not keep him very long in suspense. Before he had been many minutes in the room
the door softly opened, and Mildred stole in. His heart
leaped to see the expression on her face; the light of
love and joy shining in her eyes. He took her to his heart,
he folded his arms about her, and held her as if he would
never let her go. Never had Philip Heyward felt so
strongly the mighty and terrible strength of love.

"You are glad to see me, Philip; you have missed
me a little?" she whispered, in a voice of unutterable
content.

"So much, that it makes me afraid," he said briefly.
"It is a terrible thing for a man to love as I do, Mildred."

"Not very terrible, surely, when I love you too," she
said, smiling a little. "I think you care for me more
than you did two months ago, Philip."

"I will tell you the truth, Mildred. I asked you to be
my wife simply because I believed the time had come
when it was fitting and suitable for me to marry. You
remember I was plain with you that night."

"Yes, I remember very well; you were *very* plain
with me," she said shyly.

"I admired you and respected you more than any other woman, I said, I think, but I spoke no words of love. I was at least sincere, but not more so than I am now. You have grown into my very life, you are part of my innermost being. It would kill me to lose you now, my darling!"

It was the first time he had called her by that name, and he spoke the words with a lingering and passionate intensity, which awed while it filled her with joy unspeakable.

She crept more closely to his side, and one fair arm stole up to his tall shoulder, with light yet clinging touch.

"You remember how I said, that sad yet happy night, that perhaps some day you would understand better the needs of a woman's heart. That day is here now, Philip, and oh! my dearest, I am so happy, my heart is overcharged."

"I am not worthy of your love, Mildred," he said in a low voice, yet holding her the closer. "But I will try at least to make you a happy wife. But now, come nearer to the light. Let me look at you. Let me see whether you have spent your strength, as I feared you would, waiting on others."

"No, no, I am quite well, not even tired. They were so good to me at Kingsmead, and I was so happy among them. I shall never forget it," she said, and her eyes filled with tears. "Sit down in this chair, Philip, and let me take this stool at your feet till I tell you all about it."

9

"Not at my feet, Mildred," he said; "we can sit together on the sofa. But the maid said you had guests upstairs, I must not keep you from them."

"Oh, it is only Lady Dacre and Mrs. Monckton, mamma's friends. They came to afternoon tea, and will be going shortly. I said good-bye to them before I came down," said Mildred. Then she sat down beside him, and folded her hands on his arm.

"Tell me, Philip, why you did not come to the funeral? They all seemed to feel it very much, especially Jack."

"What I wrote was true," answered Philip, quickly. "I was so pressed by business that I couldn't possibly get away. Did they not believe it?"

"Oh yes, but I was sorry you did not come; I am very jealous of what people think and say of you, dear. Those who do not know you might judge you harshly. I sometimes think you have two distinct personalities, one for me and one for outsiders."

"I care nothing for outsiders, or their opinions, so long as *you* are pleased," he said, quickly.

"But *I* care," said Mildred, gently. "I suppose every woman is anxious that others should think well of the man she loves. It is but natural, Philip dear. I shall have occasion all my life to bless my visit to Kingsmead."

"Why so, Mildred? I should have imagined it would be dull and sad enough for you."

She looked up into his face with that pathetic mingling of wistfulness and longing, which ever awakened all the impulses of his heart.

"I have often wanted to speak to you, Philip, about

something which is very close and dear to me. I knew the time would come when I could do so quite freely. Without it there would be a shadow on my happiness."

"There shall be no shadow if I can remove it, Mildred," he said quietly.

"I know that—how thankfully I know it!" she answered, and her head drooped a little on his arm, and there was a little silence. "Long ago, Philip, when I was quite a little girl, alone, at school," she continued at length, "I used to have many strange thoughts. I used to wonder what people were born into the world for, and what was the purpose of their creation. As I grew older, and began to see and know more of the world, that question, instead of finding an easy answer, grew deeper and more perplexing every day. In the society in which I moved I saw people flitting through life like butterflies, and dying at length without leaving any mark, any influence for good behind them. There were many other things, too, which perplexed me, wrongs needing to be righted, evildoers flourishing and enjoying this life to the full, while the good bore patiently many trials. These things I could not understand. I felt so strangely in myself, too. I seemed to stand like a spectator on the outskirts watching the drama of life. But at length I too began to awaken to its reality. I began to grow sick and weary of the routine of my days. Each one passed like another, and I had done nothing either to benefit myself or any other creature. From being dissatisfied, I passed to being very unhappy. I was filled with strange longing for something I could not reach. I felt a vague sense of desolation, an aching void in my heart which nothing I had yet found could fill. I spoke to my cousin Ethel about it, and she it was who told me first that nothing but the love of God could fill the chalice of every human need. Are you cold, dear? I thought you shivered," she broke off anxiously.

"No, no—go on," said Philip Heyward in a stifled voice.

"I tried to feel good and happy, like her," she went on again. "I tried to live a better life, to keep myself aloof from the frivolities of the world. I read the Bible, and tried to pray, but none of these things brought relief. At last I gave up in despair, and it was just then that, in God's good providence, I went to Kingsmead. If I were to speak for ever, dear, I could never tell you of the boundless good I received there. It did me good just to be in the midst of a happy, united Christian family; but, as you may guess, it was to Edith herself I owed the most. To say I was amazed at her cannot express to you what I felt. She was so young, so lovely, so beloved, and so happy in every human tie, and yet she was quite willing to leave them all. To her, death indeed seemed great gain. I never realised till I was with her, that religion could indeed be a greater power than anything else on earth. The hope that was in her made her brave and strong, not only to bear uncomplainingly her great sufferings, but to soothe and calm the sorrow of those she loved here. Her utter abnegation of self was the most wonderful thing I had ever seen. And, again, there returned to me with fourfold strength the yearning for that higher life, that deeper, sweeter peace, which comes only from above; and it was Edith,

Philip, who cleared away the mist from my way, it was her hand that guided me to the light; and I saw that my mistake had been in waiting to feel some great change in myself, in trying too much to make a path for myself, and walk therein, instead of simply trusting God, and planting my feet whither He directed."

There was a brief silence. In the intensity of her earnestness, she had almost forgotten her listener, and he saw by her shining eyes and far-off expression that it was so.

"I am so glad that I can speak freely to you, Philip, because I hope and expect that you will help and guide me in the way. I think we have been too reticent towards each other—I, at least, have been, but then I am so by nature. I should not wish the slightest shadow or barrier between us, dear: I want to be able to speak to you freely on every subject. Do you understand?"

"I understand," Philip Heyward repeated, and his voice sounded hoarse and strange, even in his own ears.

"And Philip, when we are together, dear, we will work not for ourselves alone, but for Him who has so abundantly blessed us. We will try to remember that wealth is only given by God to use for Him. And so we will not only live a far happier life on earth, but we will lay up for ourselves treasures in heaven."

"I am tired, Mildred, and it is growing late," said Philip Heyward, rising heavily to his feet. "I only wanted to look at you to-night to see that you were none the worse for your visit. You will excuse me now. I will see you again, perhaps to-morrow."

Before she could recover from her astonishment, he put his arm about her, kissed her not once but many times, with strange passionate eagerness, then abruptly quitted the room. She did not know that her words, sharper than a two-edged sword, had pierced the innermost recesses of his being. She did not know how her innocent confidence had tortured him until he could bear it no longer. Truly Philip Heyward was holden with the cords of his sin.

CHAPTER FOURTEEN

THE BEGINNING OF TROUBLES.

IN the spacious and beautiful drawing-room of Phillip Heyward's house in Porchester Place sat his wife on the evening of a sweet, still October day. We will look at her for a moment, if you please, for it is night two years since we saw her last. There was but little change upon her. The figure had lost none of its former grace, although it had gained a little perhaps in dignity, much enhanced by the costly richness of her evening dress. It was a whim of Philip Heyward's that his wife's attire should be of the most expensive description; and he was equally lavish in everything, thus showing that he had cast aside the old niggardliness, and subscribed to his brother's doctrine that money is of no value until it is spent. But Dr. Heyward disposed of the balance of his large income in a different way from his brother. There were many needy ones in Linborough, ay, and out of it too, who breathed the young physician's name in accents of fervent gratitude and love, and who could tell of professional attendance, expensive medicines and nourishing food freely bestowed of sundry excursions and sojourns among health-giving hills or by the sounding sea, where strength and spirits were restored at Dr. Heyward's expense. Surely if those we love, whom God in His wisdom has removed a little while from us, are privileged to witness our actions here, the spirit of Edith Lancaster must have rejoiced over the good being done in the place where she had hoped to live a happy wife.

Philip Heyward's wife seemed to be deeply absorbed in thought. Her white hands, whereon sparkled many gems, were lightly folded on her lap, and her eyes were dreamily fixed on the dancing flames. In its perfect repose her face was graver than of yore, nay, it was almost sad. The beautiful mouth had a wistfulness in its curves, the earnest eyes seemed troubled at that moment. And yet what care could touch the heart of Philip Heyward's wife, whose lot was the envy of many of her friends? Her thoughts were flitting to and fro the brief period of her married life, and she was admitting, unconciously to herself, that though it had given her many joys, many sweet and precious things to be cherished to life's end, it had not been void of disappointment, it had held less of fullness, less of satisfaction, than she had hoped and prayed for. Why was that? Was it that her husband loved her less, that he had not fulfilled alike in spirit and letter his marriage vow? Alas! no; the cause lay even deeper than that.

Mildred Heyward had entered upon her married life, a young and inexperienced Christian full of hope and earnest resolve for the future, upheld by the expectation that her husband would be her guide and pattern, as well as her dear companion in the upward way. These hopes one by one had had to be laid aside. Ere many weeks passed, she knew that in the dearest interest of her heart, in her highest and best aspirations, the man she had married could not, and did not, sympathise. He was a churchgoer, he gave generously to every charitable object, he never refused her any sum to spend in a good cause; but of the inner life he knew and cared nothing. He was eminently a worldly man; absorbed in the business to which he devoted time and energy alike, to the exclusion of his higher good. It was by slow degrees that that certainty came home to Mildred; otherwise she could not have borne it. By slow degrees also, and almost unconsciously to herself, the well-springs of her confidence began to close against her husband. She was by nature strangely reticent; it had only been in times of deep emotion she had broached the subject of religion to him before marriage, and then she had scarcely noticed how little he had said to encourage or gladden her heart. But when he became her only and constant companion in the quiet ways of daily life, it was not long before she began to miss something in him she had expected to find. He was devotedly, passionately attached to her; kind, tender, and considerate for her at all times; denied or grudged her nothing—but that could not suffice. The earthly love alone could not satisfy, unless perfected by a touch of the divine; so, very slowly, Mildred Heyward drifted away from her husband where her religious life was concerned. She had an existence apart from his, a silent and sweet communion which he did not share. It was a great and terrible grief to her that it should be thus—a grief which could only be laid, wet with tears, at the Redeemer's feet. Surely, if it be true that the unbelieving husband is sanctified by the wife, then the earnest prayers of Mildred Heyward must, in time, bear their rich and precious fruit!

With the chiming of the jewelled clock on the mantelpiece proclaiming the hour of seven she heard her husband's key turn in the lock, and she sat up, all her listlessness gone. She loved him so dearly yet that his step had power to bring the colour to her cheek, the lustre to her eyes, and the heart-beat of joy to her breast. He came directly to the drawing-room, as was his wont, seeking her. When she turned to greet him with a lovely smile on her lips and in her eyes, she saw at once that he was worried and troubled. It seemed to her that he had aged since the morning, and that the hours of the day had added many silver threads to his dark hair.

She went to him, lifted her hands to his tall shoulders, looking into his face with tenderest solicitude.

"My dearest, what is it What has troubled you to-day? How *very* worn and anxious you look! You make me afraid."

He put his arm about her and drew her very closely to his side. The deep, careworn eyes fixed themselves upon her sweet face with an intensity of love and longing which thrilled her to the heart.

"My sweet wife, I have bad news for you to-day," he said. "Strange that I should have been so impatient to bring it home to you. Every hour has seemed a day to me to-day."

"Tell me what it is," she said, smiling slightly. "I cannot say I feel very anxious, when *you* are with me safe and well, Philip. It is some business trouble, is it not?"

"Yes, a very serious loss, my darling. The failure of a New York firm was announced by cable this afternoon. I am very deeply involved with them, and shall lose thousands."

"Is that all?" she asked, lightly. "Don't vex yourself about it, dear; we have enough and to spare. What although we had to leave this house and live in a much quieter way, when we have each other and our precious baby?"

An answering smile touched for a moment Philip Heyward's grave lips. "My darling, what a woman you are!" he said, with lingering fondness. "It will not be so bad as that; I hope and trust there will be no need to leave this house. Perhaps you may have to wear your dresses a little longer, and be disappointed of the gift I had hoped to bestow on the anniversary of our wedding-day, but that will be all."

"Then why look so grave?" she said, chidingly. "Was it a great shock to you, quite unexpected, or have you feared it for some time?"

"No; it came on me like a thunderclap. It has been a gigantic swindle; a case of carrying on an enormous concern at the public expense. They richly deserve to be tried for felony."

"Then they are much more to be pitied than we, Philip. Better a blameless loss than an unjust, unrighteous gain," she said. "Do you not think so, dear?"

"Ay, I suppose you are right," he said, a little quickly, and turned away. "How is baby to-day? Has Spencer been here?"

"Yes, he thinks him much better. I was in the nursery before I went to dress, and he was quite bright," replied Mildred. "The gong will sound in ten minutes, dear. Do you think you will have time to dress?"

"Oh, yes; I have never sat down with you in this garb yet, my darling, and I am not going to begin," he said, lightly, and left the room. Mildred stood by the table, a look of gravity stealing back to her face. She was oppressed by a vague sense of uneasiness, a prevision of trouble for which she was unable to account.

Her reverie was interrupted by a light tap at the door, and in reply to her "Come in," the under-nursemaid, a pleasant-faced girl of sixteen, appeared on the threshold.

"Please, ma'am, Mrs. Hewitt sent me to ask would you please come and look at baby? She thinks him not so well since evening came on."

In a moment every other anxiety was forgotten by the fair young mother, and she hurried to the nursery. The nurse, a kindly, responsible-looking woman, met her in the other room, which was used as a day nursery and held up a warning finger.

"He's asleep, ma'am, but he seems troubled like. I am not quite easy about him," she explained, in a whisper; "and I thought I'd like you to look at him before you went down to dinner."

Mrs. Heyward nodded, and followed the woman into the inner room. The gas was lowered, but there was sufficient light from the ruddy fire to show the little cot and its precious occupant. He was asleep, indeed, but it was an uneasy troubled slumber, and the little hands tossed restlessly outside the coverlet, and the golden head on the pillow was never a moment still. Also, the fair, round baby face, was deeply flushed, and when the mother nervously laid her cool hand on his brow, she started to find it so hot.

"There is much more fever here than there was in the afternoon, Hewitt," she whispered hurriedly. "Doctor Spencer apprehended nothing then; at least, he told me it was only a feverish cold."

The nurse shook her head.

"I'm afraid to say, ma'am, but I think it's too like scarlet fever. I've seen it too often to be mistaken."

The mother's face blanched to the very lips, and her limbs seemed to totter beneath her.

"The doctor had better be sent for at once. Elizabeth run down and see that someone goes immediately," she said, going to the door of the other room and looking at the girl; then she crossed the corridor to her husbands dressing-room and went in.

"Philip, come and see little Jack, will you? He seems worse. Hewitt thinks it is scarlet fever," she said, in a trembling whisper, for an unutterable fear had taken possession of her soul.

Philip Heyward hurriedly threw on his dressing-gown, and followed his wife to the nursery. When his eyes fell on the flushed face of his first-born, when his ear caught the hurried painful breathing, a deep shadow of anguished fear crossed his dark face.

"What did Spencer say?" he asked, turning sternly to the nurse.

"He said it was a feverish cold, sir, and would pass away in a day or two," answered the woman. "That was at three o'clock; it was about six I thought he seemed to grow worse."

"I don't believe the man knows his business," said the master, more sternly. "Go downstairs will you, and send one of the maids for Sir Andrew Beauchamp? He lives in Portman Square. My darling! do not needlessly distress yourself," he added, turning to his wife; "he may be all right."

Mildred Heyward knelt down by the little cot, and

laid her cheek against the hot hand of her darling. He stirred a little, and his lips moved. It was only the baby-cry which fell so often and so lovingly from the sweet baby lips, the only word they could utter yet, and the dearest in the English tongue to the mother's heart.

"Ma! ma! ma!"

She looked with an agony of yearning upon the child's face, at that moment forgetting the presence of her husband. Could it be that the presentiment of trouble which had been weighing upon mind and heart for days could be connected in any way with the child! "Oh, God forbid! Anything, everything, take all, but leave that!" Such was her anguished prayer.

Chapter Fifteen

"OF SUCH IS THE KINGDOM OF HEAVEN."

HEWITT'S fears proved only too well grounded. Late in the evening Sir Andrew Beauchamp, the great London doctor whose name had so puzzled Tom Lancaster, arrived at Philip Heyward's house in Porchester Place. After one glance at the child, he pronounced that scarlet fever, just then an epidemic among children in the western and southern districts, had taken a serious hold upon the system. Sir Andrew was a man who never gilded his pill, and who was sometimes blamed for the blunt abruptness with which he announced hopeless or dangerous illness. But, at any rate, unflinching candour spared many a heart the agony of suspense, the vanity of a delusive hope.

He did not prolong his visit, for his time was precious indeed. As he went downstairs with the master of the house he inquired who was their family physician "Spencer, of Cadogan Place," Philip Heyward answered. "But if you would undertake the case, Sir Andrew, I should regard it as a personal favour. I need scarcely say that where my son is concerned, money is no object to me."

Sir Andrew shook his head.

"I am simply a consulting physician, Mr. Heyward, and had I not expected to meet your medical man here, probably, I should not have come. I dare make no exception, or I should be wholly unable to overtake a tithe of the engagements which would be forced upon me," he answered, bluntly. "But if you like, I will see Spencer here in the morning."

With that concession Philip Heyward was obliged to be content. Mildred Heyward did not quit the nursery that night. Even when assured that her presence was wholly unnecessary, that it could do no good, when entreated to husband her strength for the watching which might be needed, she just shook her head, and sat with her yearning eyes fixed on the child's flushed face, and one continuous agonising prayer on her heart.

For many days a great shadow lay on the house in Porchester Place. Servants slipped about on tip-toe, noiselessly shutting doors, and talking in whispers, often with tears in their eyes; for the bright, happy, winsome baby had been loved by them all. Lady Vere went and came between Curzon Street and Porchester Place, but she was of little real help; and her loud whisper and rustling skirts were more than her daughter's over-strained nerves could bear. Mrs. St. John and Ethel came up from Finsbury Park, and the latter remained. In the house of sickness or mourning Ethel St. John was at home, and invaluable. The fever was virulent, and when it ran its course, left the little frame far spent. There were moments when they had to bend down to feel the heart pulsations, for he lay so still that they thought him dead.

"Send for Jack, Philip," Mildred said, one morning. "Perhaps he may do no good; but I should like him to see baby, it would just satisfy me." Mechanically Philip Heyward left the house and went to the nearest post-office to telegraph for his brother. He moved, acted, and

felt like a man in a dream. He heard them speak of the
hopelessness of the child's sickness without comprehending what they meant. The love which Philip Heyward
had for his first-born son was no ordinary parental love.
It was a deep, engrossing passion, a species of idolatry,
which had a vein of selfishness in it. The possibility of
the child's death had never once occurred to him; and
even now, when the grim angel stood with dark wings
outspread over his home, he refused to give up hope of
life. After the first agony of apprehension, of bitter,
rebellious pain, the mother's heart had been stilled
by the loving touch of a merciful Father's hand. It was
in this hour of hardest trial that the faith and hope that
was in her sustained her fainting heart. She could leave
the child with God; and so, because she was stayed by
her faith, she moved, an angel of help, in the stricken
household; and she whom it touched more nearly and
dearly than any was the calmest of them all.

Doctor Heyward came to town that day by the afternoon train, and arrived at his brother's house about
half-past four. Philip, watching for him (for business was
neglected in these sad days), met him in the hall.

They shook hands in silence.

"How is Mildred?" was Jack's first question as they
entered the dining-room together.

"Wonderfully well," Philip answered, in a muffled
voice. "She bears it better than I. You will do what
you can for the child, Jack?"

"When men like Beauchamp and Spencer have
failed, Phil, what can I do?" Jack asked sadly. "The
poor little chap! I never saw a finer child. I think I
love him, Phil, nearly as well as you."

"He bears your name," Philip said, with his hand on the bell-rope; and when the servant entered, he added, "Tell your mistress Doctor Heyward has come, and ask her if we may come up now."

Before many minutes passed, she returned to say that Mrs. Heyward would like them to come up at once.

Mildred met them at the door of the day-nursery, and when Jack kissed her in silence, she looked up with the faintest glimmer of a smile in her wistful eyes.

"We could not be content until Uncle Jack had seen our pet," she said, a little unsteadily. "I am glad you have come. He is not asleep; come in."

Very lightly Doctor Heyward stepped into the inner room and across to the bed. The woeful change upon the child whom he had last seen in the flush of health and baby-beauty made his heart ache.

He stooped down and addressed the little one by his name, but though the golden lashes stirred a little on the white cheek, the blue, veined lids were not uplifted. Strength was too far spent even for that exertion. But the little fingers moved, and when they were taken in Uncle Jack's strong, kind grasp, they rested there content.

He felt the feeble, irregular flutter of the pulse against his palm, and his heart yearned over the child with an unspeakable yearning. He would have willingly given ten years of his life to be able to save him for his father and mother; but now human skill was of no avail.

They stood in absolute silence for a few minutes, and then he turned to Mildred and slightly shook his head. She understood that gesture, and slipped away to the outer room. They joined her there after a little, and

Jack laid his kind hand on her shoulder where she stood, with her head bowed on her breast.

"God knows best, Mildred; either way it will be well with the child," he said quietly.

With a deep groan, Philip Heyward turned on his heel and left the room.

"I have given him up, Jack; He knows at what cost," she answered, in a whisper. "It is a fearful thing to be a mother."

"God knows that also, my sister," Jack made answer tenderly. "But, after all, it will only forge another link 'twixt earth and heaven; and the parting is but for a little while."

A quick sob caught the mother's breath, and the tears came. Then Jack stole away, knowing they brought healing with them. He found Philip in the drawing-room pacing up and down the floor, with a hard, set expression on his face.

"You can do nothing for him, I suppose?" he said, quickly, when Jack entered.

"Nothing. That extreme prostration can have but one end. Eric was healthy but not very robust, Phil, and the fever must have taken a terrible hold on the system."

"And I am to stand by and see the child die!" said Philip, with an intensity of bitterness which almost startled Jack.

"It will just be a closing of the eyes, a falling asleep," he said, gently. "Mildred has given him up. She can say, even already, 'It is well,' and she is his mother."

"I cannot understand her," said Philip, with bitter impatience. "Give him up! why, I'd give up anything

rather than the child. Why should the most precious
thing a man has be torn from him ruthlessly like this?"

Jack shook his head.

"I know all you feel; I have experienced it before you;
but, believe me, the time will come when you will be
glad the child is safe. After all, he is spared much trouble,
for what is life but trouble here?"

"People speak about the love of God; but what kind
of a love is it which can be so cruel? The child has only
lived long enough to make himself a necessity in our
lives, and then he is taken away. There is something
far amiss in such dealing with men," said Philip, rebel-
liously.

"There must be a purpose in it, though it is hid from
us," said Jack. "When everything goes smoothly with
us, I think we forget the highest purposes of life, and so
sorrow is sent to bring us back to the narrow way."

"You have grown quite a philosopher," interrupted
Philip sarcastically, and abruptly turned and left the
room. The words had touched something in his heart—
a chord of memory, and slumbering conscience was
awakened once more. Could it be that one by one the
things he prized most on earth would be wrested from
him in punishment for his sin? Would the avenger be
relentless, and pause not until he was left desolate and
ruined on the face of the earth? Already a great portion
of his wealth had taken wings, and now his idolised
child was dying. These thoughts occupied the mind of
Philip Heyward through the silent watches of the night
which he spent alone in the darkened library, alone with
his accusing conscience, face to face with the dark and
blameworthy past.

At the dawn a servant came hurrying in search of him—Her tearful eye and trembling lip proclaimed her message before she spoke. "Oh, sir, will you come up, please? the baby, sir——"

He strode past her, and in two seconds had entered the room where the child lay. The nurse stood weeping at the other side of the bed; the stricken mother, with her head on the pillow beside the golden one, knelt in prayer.

And the child himself? The sweet son of peace and joy, who had spread his wings for a little space over an earthly home, growing weary, had plumed them for flight to a fairer, sunnier clime. For "of such is the kingdom of heaven."

Chapter Sixteen

DARK HOURS

WITH her own hands Mildred Heyward dressed her little one for his last sleep; the nurse, who handed the garments to her one by one, marvelled at her calmness. It was not the stony calm of despair, but a sweet serious-ness which betokened a heart at rest; and it was at rest, because she had but given the child, lent to her a little while, back to God.

"Oh, ma'am, he looks so lovely; I never saw a dearer, sweeter baby," said Hewitt, through her tears. "And so natural-like. It is hard to believe him dead."

"Don't speak of him as dead, Hewitt," said the mother, in gentle rebuke. "He has only gone away to a dearer, happier home."

"Yes, yes, ma'am, I know; but still we'll miss the precious child sorely," said Hewitt, weeping still. The thought of the empty nursery, the stillness which must now reign in the house, touched the mother's heart, and her lip quivered. Then it was that her thoughts turned to her husband, bearing his sorrow somewhere alone. She stole away downstairs, looked into the drawing-room to find it empty, and then turned her steps to the library. It was very dreary there, for the fire had long since died in the grate, and the wintry dawn which crept chilly in through the half-drawn venetians, only served to make the place look more desolate and cold. It also was empty. Where, then, had her husband gone?

The housemaid entering just then to perform her household duties answered her unspoken question.

"The master has gone out, ma'am; I heard him go out by the hall door just—just after——"

The girl paused and her mistress at once understood. he had gone out to fight his battle away from every eye.

Now that all was over, the overtaxed strength gave way, and Mildred felt the need of rest. So she went upstairs again, and after another lingering look at her darling, went away to bed, and at once fell into the heavy dreamless sleep of utter exhaustion. About nine o'clock, the usual breakfast hour, Philip Heyward returned to his home. He found Ethel in the morning-room, ready to minister to his wants, and from her he learned that his wife had gone to bed. It was a poor pretence of eating Philip Heyward made that morning, and Ethel's gentle heart bled for him. She never felt quite at home with her cousion's husband; she was rather in awe of him, he was so reserved and still, so unlike his brother in every way. But he must be a good man, else Mildred could not love him so dearly; thus Ethel reasoned, chiding herself for her vague distrust.

When the meal was over, Philip Heyward drawn by some magnet, against his inclination, went upstairs to the room where lay his sleeping child in the pleasant nursery. The morning light was subdued, and he had to draw the curtain of the cot a little aside before he could see the baby's face. Oh, but it was fair and sweet and peaceful to look upon! The sight of that heavenly calm was sufficient to still even the wildest storm of rebellious grief. So natural, indeed, did the sweet face appear that it was hard to believe him dead. There was a great profusion of flowers about the bed; blossoms as fair and delicate as the babe himself; and on the wall just above the bed was suspended by a white satin cord a scroll, exquisitely painted, and bearing these words in letters of gold: "Of such is the kingdom of heaven." Philip Heyward started at sight of these words. He had never seen the thing in the nursery before, though in all likelihood it had been there for many a day. Why should that sentence, that most familiar of Bible texts, strike him so strangely to-day? "Of such is the kingdom of heaven." He left the house by and by, after ascertaining that his wife still slept, and turned his steps towards St. Paul's Churchyard; yet still the words haunted him, coming between him and his business thoughts; he read them in his letters, saw the words in the very figures of his ledger. "Of such is the kingdom of heaven." He remembered too the words of another verse, which said: "Whosoever shall not receive the kingdom of God as a little child, he shall not enter therein."

If these words were true then indeed his child was lost to him for ever. The portals, which had opened so gladly that day to admit the pure spirit of the little one, would be closed against him; for elsewhere in the Bible he had read that there is no admittance therefore whosoever loveth or maketh a lie. What had his life been these past years but a living lie? What was it now but a daily, hourly deception practised upon the world, and upon the heart of his innocent and trusting wife? All day Philip Heyward remained in his room at the warehouse, denying himself to all who came asking for him; and even the most frivolous and thoughtless of the young lads in the outer office hushed their idle chatter, knowing that the little heir was dead, and feeling a vague sympathy and respect for their austere master's grief. They did not dream of the fierce warfare being waged in that inner room, of the sharp conflict between good and evil; little recked they of the issues which hung trembling in the balance. He waited till all the employees had left the place, and himself locked up the premises for the night. Then he emerged into the sweet starlight of the clear October night, and walked with swift step away from, instead of towards, his home. Passing along Fleet Street, he turned into the Temple Gardens. Oh, but it was quiet and refreshing in the green enclosure that autumn night! Every footstep sent its echoes reverberating through the dim cloisters, making the contrast between the roar of the busy world outside almost painful. Philip Heyward looked round him with a troubled, almost bewildered air, as if struggling to remember what had brought him there. As his eye fell suddenly upon the bench under the trees, where once before the tempter had entered into possession of his soul, he shuddered, and turning abruptly on his heel, quitted the place. Hailing a passing hansom he drove home to Porchester Place. As he took off his overcoat in the hall he heard voices upstairs, and beckoning to a servant, crossing to the dining-room, asked who was in the drawing-room.

"Lady Vere, and Mrs. Heyward from Linborough, sir, are there with Miss St. John," she answered. "Dr. Heyward arrived too, sir, but I think he went out to meet you, as he asked very particularly if you walked home, and how you usually came."

"I drove home," answered the master briefly. "Is your mistress up?"

"Oh yes, sir, but she will not come down to dinner to-night. She is sitting up in her dressing-room," said the girl. "I took up a cup of tea a little while ago, and she asked if you had come home."

"Ah! When will dinner be ready?"

"At half-past seven, sir—the usual hour."

"Do you know if the ladies intend to remain all night?"

"Yes, sir; Mrs. Heyward ordered rooms to be prepared for them, but I think Dr. Heyward returns to Linborough by the late train. That was why he was so anxious to see you," said the girl, and wondered why her master looked a little annoyed. He passed her and went straight upstairs to the drawing-room. While he was speaking to the ladies there, Jack returned and the gong sounded almost immediately. Philip Heyward started when he heard it, and for the first time was conscious of his negligent attire. But, as Jack himself was not in evening dress, he asked the ladies to excuse him, and offered his mother-in-law his arm.

None of them marvelled at the grave reticence exhibited by the master of the house, nor took particular heed of his absent manner at the table. In the sad circumstances it was only natural. Immediately after dinner, Doctor Heyward had to leave for the train, and his brother walked with him to the station at Charing Cross. There was very little said; all Jack's sympathy had been expressed in the glance of the eye, the fervent grip of the hand, and the deep "God bless you!" with which he had greeted him an hour ago.

"I'll be up again, old fellow, you know. When is the—you know what I mean?" he broke off suddenly, for to Jack the word "funeral" was distasteful in the extreme.

"The funeral? I don't know; I have not thought about it," replied Philip, vaguely, as if an entirely new idea had just been presented to his mind.

"Mildred spoke of Friday afternoon, and she would like the little one to sleep beside his grandfather," said Jack.

"At Kingsmead, you mean?"

"No, no; his other grandfather, Sir James Wyatt, you know. He is buried at Hadley, where the family live," said Jack, looking compassionately at his brother, who evidently did not yet realise his loss.

"I'll see about it. I'll speak to Mildred to-night, and let you know some time to-morrow," said Philip; then: "Is this your train? Well, good night."

"Good night," said Jack, with another fervent grip; "I am very sorry for you, old chap; but you are not desolate when you have Mildred left."

It was nine o'clock when Philip Heyward once more entered his home, and after removing his greatcoat, he went upstairs, passing the drawing-room, and entered his wife's dressing-room. She was sitting in a low chair on the hearth, her magnificent hair unbound, and falling like a cloud about her shoulders. She turned her head at her husband's entrance, and he was quick to note that her face equalled the whiteness of the spotless dressing-gown she wore. Her lips quivered, and she extended tremulous hands to him; her whole attitude was one of the intensest love and longing.

"Oh, Philip! why did you stay so long? The day has has been so long, so long without you!"

He took the pale, slender hands in a grip which hurt, and pressed them to his lips. She looked at him almost fearfully, missing the accustomed kiss, the words of love, which, hitherto, she had never looked for in vain, and for which all day her heart had been hungering in its desolation. She released one hand, and passed it tenderly across his furrowed brow; ready in her unselfishness to administer the comfort she so sorely needed herself.

"My dearest, we must not bear it alone, away from each other," she said, unsteadily. "We have each other left; and though our darling will not return to us, we shall go to him. What is it, Philip? Don't look at me so strangely. Hold me close, as you used to do. My husband, I am afraid!"

He released the trembling hands; he resolutely curbed the impulse which bade him passionately respond to her appeal. The hour had come for him to make confession of his sin to the woman he had wronged, the confession which might, nay, would be the death-blow to her love. He knew, none better, that it was cruel to strike the blow to-night, to inflict so terrible a pain on her already riven heart; but he knew also that to wait for a more convenient season, ay, to tarry even until to-morrow, was but playing into the hands of the tempter, before whom he had so miserably fallen before. He knew by experience that he dared not trust himself. Whatever the cost, the story of his temptation and his sin must be told to-night.

And yet, never had his wife, the darling of his heart,

been so dear as now; never had her clinging love seemed so unutterably precious a thing as at this moment, when he was about to cast it away from him for ever.

"Philip, dear, looking at you, I am afraid," she said. "Oh, my darling, surely this sorrow is not going to estrange your heart from me, the mother of your little angel child?"

She rose as she spoke, and fixing her pathetic, wistful eyes on his face, laid a pleading hand on his arm. He turned to her, and kissed her forehead almost as one might kiss the face of the dead.

"Sit down, Mildred," he said, and gently placed her in a chair. "I have a story to tell, which may God give you strength to bear."

Chapter Seventeen

ERRING, BUT FORGIVEN

MILDRED HEYWARD leaned back in her chair, and fixed her wide, wistful eyes full upon her husband's face. In her heart of hearts she feared that this bereavement had unhinged him. Yet when he spoke presently, his tone was calm and measured; his face, though grave, resolute and undisturbed.

"I must ask you to go back with me a very long time, Mildred," he began, not looking at her, but keeping his eyes fixed on the glowing fire. "Back to my boyhood, so that you may better understand the story I have to tell. I was always a strange and miserable-minded child; even in the days when my brother and I played together in the nursery and the garden at Kingsmead Vicarage. When we went to school I made no companons; I lived an isolated, lonely life, while Jack was simply idolised. I do not remember the time when I did not love money. The childish pence given to me by friends were precious to me, not for the childish delights they could procure, but simply because I could look at them day by day, and feel that I had money of my own. I never spent anything, nor would I give it to Jack to spend. Many a quarrel we had as boys over it, and he would call me selfish, and greedy, and miserly; but what did I care? I knew that money meant power, and that it's possessor was a more important personage than he who lacked it. Very early I made up my mind to become a merchant. My favourite literature was stories or biographies of men who had grown rich by their own exertions, and whose great wealth had obtained for them positions of trust and importance in their day and generation. I resolved that such should be my lot in life; and for that I laboured and saved from my boyhood upward. I think you know that soon after my father's death I came to London, and entered the firm of which I am now the head. It was not long before my employer recognised in me a different order of being from the usual mercantile apprentice. He watched me with observant eye, and seeing I was likely to suit him in many ways, for he was himself of penurious and miserly habits, he steadily advanced me step by step, until I became, while still very young, his managing and confidential clerk. He had no secrets from me, and though I learned that certain departments of his business were not conducted on strictly honourable principles, I experienced no difficulty in stilling the voice of conscience with the sophism that it was only a shrewd and perfectly legitimate way of earning the largest profits. Fortunately, as I thought, for me, my mother had not hitherto required any help from her sons. She had been comfortably left, and was able to give Jack the necessary training to fit him for the medical profession, for which he very early showed a predilection. But during the last years of his studies, a mining concern, in which my mother's chief means were invested, turned out a complete swindle, and she lost all. I was perfectly able to help her, had I been so inclined; but I refused, or, at least, did not offer to do so, and she was too proud to ask. For such a lack of filial duty I have no excuse; I am simply telling you the truth. Jack did not spare me, however, but his plain speaking had no effect whatsoever on me. I laughed contemptuously at his high-sounding, but, as I thought, empty boasts of what he would do for our mother; and when I heard that he had actually decided to start the practice of his profession in Linborough, where he now is, I was perfectly astounded. I never thought the lad had so much real pluck in him; but he proved himself a reproach as well as an example to me, who ought to have been an example to him. In August of 1872, my mother and Jack set up house in Linborough, and I was left to my money-getting in London.

"For considerably more than a year before his death, my employer's health had been visibly declining. He was suffering from some internal malady which could not be cured. It was in the month of December that he was finally laid aside." Here Philip Heyward paused a moment, but did not trust himself to look at his wife's face. But he was perfectly conscious that she had leaned forward in her chair, and was listening with intense strained eagerness to every word which fell from his lips, fearing she knew not what.

"One day he was at the office; the next morning a messenger came, summoning me to his residence in Cecil Street, at once. I went, and found him in bed; and though I had had comparatively little experience of sickness, I saw perfectly well that his life would not be much prolonged. He talked a good deal on business matters, and when I was with him later in the day he told me some particulars of his family history with which I had previously been unacquainted. The relations between us had never been more than that of master and servant; and I was not curious by nature, or I might have learned his story long ago. I knew he lived alone, and fancied him without kindred in the world, until he told me that day that it was possible his only sister, who had made an early and imprudent marriage, for which she was disowned by her family, might still be living. It appeared that she had been in difficulties at one time, and had applied in vain to her brother for assistance. Since that time he had heard nothing of her except that her husband, a singer, Rudolph Bernstein by name, had died in obscurity and poverty in a poor quarter of the city. The old man seemed haunted by reproach for his hardness of heart, and told me he was now anxious to make what reparation lay in his power. Too feeble, and far spent to undertake the task himself, he laid upon me, his confidential and trusted clerk, the fulfilment of his last wish and dying charge, which was to find Rudolph Bernstein's widow or children, and to make them legatees of his wealth. He told me first that Tomlinson & Hodge, od Chancery Lane, had drawn up a will for him some months previously, which left his entire fortune, with some triffling exceptions to me. However, when death was at hand, he saw more clearly that his own kith and kin had a nearer and more urgent claim upon him, which conscience would not allow him to set aside. At his request, I sent for the lawyer to draw up the new will, which left his wealth to Mary Gooderich or her heirs, with the exception of five thousand pounds to me, in payment for the trouble I should have in instituting the search for them. Tomlinson was out of Town, and when he arrived late in the evening Mr. Gooderich was dead. Do you follow me clearly?"

He paused again, but now his wife's white face was hidden in her hand, and she was sitting motionless as a statue.

"Perhaps I need not tell you what followed. My sin must be shaping itself in your mind. The devil came to me with a horrible temptation, and, hesitating a moment, I was lost. I swear to you, Mildred, that it was upon the impulse of a moment, not by premeditated act, that I committed myself by allowing the lawyer to address me as the heir to the old man's wealth. I seemed to drift with some black and sweeping tide, against which my better self was powerless to struggle. I subscribed to the only written will and testament of Christopher Gooderich, and entered upon the possession of his wealth, which was no more mine than it was the lawyer's who congratulated me as a lucky and enviable man. Let no man think that ill-gotten wealth can be enjoyed with impunity. No sooner had I taken the fatal step than I wished it a thousand times recalled. I was a miserable conscience-stricken man, whose life was utterly void of brightness or happiness, until your love, of which I was and am so utterly unworthy, shed its light and radiance on my heart."

Philip Heyward's voice, which had never hitherto betrayed a tremor or changed its tone, faltered now.

"I suppose it was because I lived so much alone, and because my life was so still and monotonous, so little stirred by any of the sweeter sympathies common to other men, that love took so intense and absorbing a hold upon my heart. It grew upon me day by day, as you know, until it became my very life; and loving you so, knowing your worth, your purity, your Christ-like innocence and

unselfishness, the past years have been a very martyrdom
because of the contrast ever present to me between your
soul and my own. It was not the least bitter part of the
sting that you believed in me so implicitly, that you
loved me with such a boundless and perfect trust. Perhaps
if I had loved you less, or if I had doubted for a moment
your love for me, I should have made my confession long
ago. It has been on my lips a hundred, nay a thousand
times, and as many times forced back. My life was so
barren before you blessed it with your love, that I could
not contemplate the loss of your respect and esteem (the
sure foundations of love) with calmness. And so all these
years I have deceived you. I have spent lavishly the
wealth which was not mine to touch; I have lived at the
expense of the widow and the orphan, who may be
destitute for lack of the gold which is theirs by right. The
burden has lately become more than I can bear. Mildred,
your grief over the child's death may be deep, but it
cannot equal mine, for I know that I am parted from
him for ever. The heaven to which he has gone will
gladly welcome you, but in that city there will be no
place for such as I. I have no more to say. I do not,
because I dare not, ask you to forgive me, only I would
ask that your judgment upon me may be a little tempered
by the thought of my unworthy yet undying love for you.
If my punishment at your hands be separation from you,
I cannot blame you. I have forfeited all claim upon your
consideration or generous kindness. Whatever happens
I have no right to say my punishment is greater than
I deserve."

In the dead silence which ensued, Philip Heyward
sat down and covered his face with his hands. He sat

thus for a long time, and when he looked up it was to find himself alone.

And Mildred? There was someone else in the nursery besides the quiet sleeper in the baby's cot—a tall figure in white pacing between the window and the locked door, with hands clenched together, and the anguish of a great agony setting its deep pain-lines on the colourless face. Thank God! such moments do not occur often in a life-time, and even then only in the experience of a very few. The baby's death was nothing to this abrupt and awful shattering of her idol, this sudden and unlooked-for storm which shook the very foundations of her faith in things human and Divine. To a woman of Mildred Heyward's calibre this blow was one of peculiar intensity and bitterness. She had been so proud of her husbands business life, of his upright dealings, his keen sense of honour in the ordinary transactions betwixt man and man; indeed, she had hoped that that very integrity would help him nearer the Christian life. And the straw to which she had clung was swept away at once and for ever! She was not conscious of any feeling of bitterness against him, only a strange, sad wonder, a vast and bound-less pity for the man who had so woefully erred. But she had felt that she must be alone for a little to think it out, to frame words with which to answer the miserable story. So he had stolen away to bear the first and keenests pain alone with God and her sleeping child. She paused once beside the bed, and looking down upon the sweet face, breathed a passionate thanksgiving that *he* at least would never know of his father's sin. She felt a great envy of that untroubled slumber; after all, death was a kind, kind friend; for life was a thorny and stony way, full of pitfalls and painful deeps for weary human feet.

She unlocked the nursery door by-and-by and stepped out into the corridor. She met Mrs. Heyward there on her way to her own room, for it was now nearly midnight. The elder woman started at sight of the figure in white, and gently touched her arm. "My dear, I thought you were in bed. It is not good for you to stay so much in there," she said, kindly, pointing to the nursery door.

"I know; I am going now—good night," Mildred whispered back and stole away to her dressing-room Mrs. Heyward proceeded upstairs, deeply concerned for her son's wife, who looked painfully ill.

Mildred found her husband where she had left him, a motionless and desolate figure sitting with bowed head beside the dying fire. So lightly did she cross the room that he was unaware of her entrance, of her presence even, until the gentle hand fell upon his shoulder.

"Philip, I am here, I am come back; God has taken all the bitterness out of my heart. My darling, in this hour of bitter trial, who is to help and comfort you but your wife?"

Philip Heyward flung up his head, and looked at the face bending over him, with a questioning, almost incredulous gaze. It was deadly pale; there were great purple rims about the eyes and mouth which had not been there an hour ago. But never in all the time he had known and loved that face had he seen such a look upon it. It was Divine in its compassion, its sympathy, its love. A tremor shook the strong man's frame, and falling on his knees, he kissed the very hem of her garment; while tears such as are wrung from the innermost heart fell upon her feet.

"Mildred! wife—wife!" he said, hoarsely. "There is no difference in your voice. If God and you have forgiven me, surely there is hope yet for my despairing, my almost lost soul!"

"The Master whom I profess to serve is a God of mercy and love, my husband; therefore, can I withhold my poor forgiveness?" she said, tremulously. "I thank Him that we may still atone; that it may not yet be too late to make reparation to the wronged. You will set about it at once, my husband?"

"God helping me," said Philip Heyward, brokenly and humbly. "My wife, can it be you will still permit me to call you by that precious name, in spite of the great and irreparable wrong I have done you?"

"Not irreparable, please God," said Mildred Heyward, and she folded her hands on her husband's arm and looked into his face. "Kiss me, Philip; we will begin a new life together above our baby's grave. I do not grudge him now, since I see so plainly what his death was sent to accomplish."

Boundless, indeed, is the depth and unselfishness of a woman's love!

CHAPTER EIGHTEEN

MERCY, NOT JUDGMENT

THE task of discovering the widow or children of Rudolph Bernstein was one of peculiar difficulty. Yet the very fact that Mary Gooderich's husband had once been before the public as a singer and musician suggested means whereby his later circumstances and the subsequent fate of the widow might be learned. Before taking into his confidence any detective or lawyer, Philip Heyward made some inquiries himself. He went to the *Times* office, and in a file of that newspaper, dated February, 1852, came upon an announcement, stating that Rudolph Bernstein, the favourite tenor, would sing at a morning concert at Willis's Rooms. Turning to a later date, November, 1856, Philip Heyward's eye was arrested by another announcement, the wording of which indicated a change, and not for the better, in the position and circumstances of the singer. He was not now alluded to as the popular tenor; but the brief paragraph simply stated that M. Rudolph Bernstein was open to engagements, and would also give lessons in singing, as well as pianoforte and violin tuition, at his residence, 4, Dynevor Terrace, Bayswater. Philip Heyward carefully noted the address, and went straight from the *Times* office to Bayswater. Dynevor Terrace at one time, though certainly much farther back than 1856, might have been a genteel and even rather stylish locality, but it was now a dingy, shabby, poor-looking row of houses, much shut in and obscured by the many new streets and imposing buildings which had sprung up all around it. The houses were brick, blackened and discoloured by the smoke from a neighbouring chimney stack, and the poor little gardens before the front windows were pitiful to look upon in their stunted and barren growth. Number four was peculiarly dirty and neglected-looking, the muslin curtains and blinds at the windows being sadly smoke-begrimed, and considerably the worse for wear. The brass knocker refused to perform its function but Philip Heyward applied his knuckles to the door, and sent a hundred echoes sounding through the house. After waiting in vain for about five minutes he knocked again, and then a grey head peered suspiciously over the under curtain at one of the lower windows. After considerable shuffling about and shutting of doors within, the key was turned in the outer door, and it was gingerly opened about three inches.

"What do you want?" queried a shrill voice. "There's nobody's life worth insuring here, and we don't read any books, and I've no old clothes to sell."

"I'm neither an insurance agent, nor a book canvasser, nor a dealer in old clothes, ma'am," said Philip Heyward. "I am a gentleman seeking information regarding a family who once resided here—the family of Rudolph Bernstein, the singer."

"Eh, what? you don't say so!" queried the uncourteous dame, in a very astonished voice. "If that's your business I daresay you might come in, and I'll tell you all I know." Philip Heyward would much have preferred to hold their interview in the purer air of the doorstep; however, he thanked her, and accepted her invitation to enter the unwholesome dwelling. She ushered him across the small square hall into a sitting-room on her left, a dingy place, smelling of moth and dust and general decay. The furniture was worn and shabby to a degree the whole appearance of the place unpleasant to a fastidious eye. The individual who admitted Philip Heyward, and who seemed to be the sole occupant of the house, was an old woman, with a withered, weird-looking face, in which gleamed a pair of very bright black eyes, which she keenly fixed on her visitor's face as she folded her arms preparatory to imparting the information he desired.

"Are you any relation of the Bernsteins?" she queried by way of introduction.

"No, but I am interested in them. Can you tell me how long it is since they occupied this house?—or perhaps they are here still?" he said, as if struck by a sudden thought.

"They never *occupied* this house; that is, they were never tenants of it," said the old woman. "Mr. Bernstein and his family boarded with me over five years."

"There *was* a family then?" he said inquiringly.

"Yes, two. They boarded with me, as I said, sir, and the master in this house died; the only one that's left now is young Walter, who is trying to earn his bread and butter painting pictures and drawing designs somewhere in the city," said the old woman, mournfully.

"You see, sir, when Mr. Bernstein came here first he

seemed pretty well off, and his wife, as gentle and sweet a creature as ever drew the breath of life, and far too good for him, *I* always said, seemed to be happy and content. She brought one baby with her, and the other was born in this very house; but it was a delicate thing, a girl, and nobody was surprised that it died before it could set its feet to the ground. Bernstein was no great things; being a foreigner and a singer, I suppose it wasn't to be expected of him; anyway he wasn't very good to his poor wife, who, I could see very well, belonged to the better class. He drank so deeply that he was hardly ever fit for his duties, and so the few pupils he had soon left him. Before they had been two years here he died in a fit, brought on by excessive drinking. The poor young creature was left nearly destitute, but I had got so fond of her and the boy that I never pressed her for the rent, but always said she could pay it back when she grew rich. She took in some pupils for music and drawing, for she was accomplished herself, and she managed to scrape up an existence. But when she saw that there was little hope of her ever being able to pay the rent of my rooms, she left, and went into the city. It was against my heart to let them go away, but I was a lone creature myself, with very little but my rooms to depend on; but I never lost sight of her all the weary years she struggled to bring up her boy respectably. I don't suppose you, sir, can have any idea what that means for a woman in a great city. Anyhow she managed it, though Heaven alone knows how; and just when her son had grown to manhood and was able to work for her she slipped away, worn out and old before her time with the life she had led; and though I couldn't help crying, sir, when I went to see her before she died, I knew she was going away to a better rest and a kinder world than this had ever been."

"How long is it since she died?" asked Philip Heyward, huskily.

"Not long," but dear me! it *is* four years past last month, sir—how the time flies!"

"And the young man, where can he be found?"

"At his lodgings in Red Lion Court—a poor little place, sir—perhaps you know it? opening off Red Lion Street. He comes here always on Saturday afternoons when he isn't down at Hampden Court seeing the pictures. He is such a man for pictures, sir; and I know if he'd had the chance he'd have been a great painter himself. He isn't the same lad since his mother died; it took all the heart out of him, you see; he had nobody but her, and he just worshipped her. May I never see a sadder sight than him sitting in his desolation that day she died!"

"Red Lion Court; any number?" said Philip Heyward with strange abruptness; "or is there a landlady?"

"Yes, a Mrs. Fitz-James, an Irish woman, kind like all her country-folk; and you'll find him in after five at night. He's a draughtsman's clerk at some warehouse near the river."

"I am infinitely obliged to you, ma'am, for the kind manner in which you have given me so much valuable information," said Philip Heyward, taking up his hat. "I am sure it will be a satisfaction to you to learn that in doing so you have done the young man good."

"Do you say so? Do tell me, sir, if you are any relation; I did so often wonder who or what his dear mother's relatives were, though of course I never expected Bernstein to have any," she said, with quiet scorn.

"No, I am no relation, but I am seeking the young man because he is the rightful heir to a large fortune left him by his uncle."

The good soul's face beamed with satisfaction. In spite of her grimy and unprepossessing appearance, she had evidently a kind and generous heart.

"That's the best news I've heard this many a day. Well, well, he'll make a good use of the money; he is a deserving lad, and has been trained in a good school. Well, good-day to you, sir; I'm glad I've been of use to you," she said, smiling, as her fingers closed over the glittering coins dropped into her palm.

It was only two o'clock when Philip Heyward returned to the city, but he felt no inclination to go home. He walked from the station to St. Paul's and remained in his office until the great bell proclaimed the hour of five. He was about to leave the place then, when he suddenly remembered that as the young man was employed in an office near the river, he could not possibly reach his lodgings much before six. Therefore, he waited till all the clerks had left; and when he passed out of the warehouse himself it was twenty minutes to six. He walked with quick, nervous steps along the crowded thoroughfare, turned into Chancery Lane, and then through Holborn to Red Lion Street. Red Lion Court was easily found, and when Philip Heyward saw the place where

Christopher Gooderich's rightful heir had his abode his
heart smote him anew with a terrible remorse.

A ragged urchin amusing himself by turning somer-
saults in the gutter readily responded to the gentlemans
inquiry regarding Mrs. Fitz-James, and pointed with
grimy forefinger to three little windows above a green-
grocer's shop. The entrance to the house was by a low
doorway, and up a somewhat tumbledown inside stair.
There was only one door on the landing, at which Philip
Heyward knocked, and it was at once opened by a tiny,
middle-aged woman, who betrayed her nationality in
her broad, humorous-looking face and dark eyes, even
before she uttered a word.

"Yes, Misther Bernstein is in; will the gintleman
kindly step into the sitting-room?" she said, with a sweeping curtsey, for it was not often so distinguished-looking
a visitor came to Mrs. Fitz-James's humble abode.

It was a small but neat and comfortable little room
into which he was ushered, and a figure rose from a
primitive-looking easle in the window and turned in
astonishment at the announcement of a visitor. Philip
Heyward looked keenly at the young man, endeavouring
to trace in face and figure some slight resemblance to
Christopher Gooderich. But in vain. The slight, delicate-
looking face, the fair, sweet, almost womanish face, the
lustrous but melancholy eyes, the curling golden hair,
were as different as could well be from the remembered
personal appearance of Christopher Gooderich.

"Mr. Walter Bernstein?" Philip Heyward said, in
low, nervous tones.

"At your service, sir," replied the young man, both face and voice betraying his wonder and surprise. "Will you please sit down?"

"Thank you; not now," said Philip Heyward, in brief, business-like tones. "Are you at leisure for the rest of the evening? Could you accompany me to my home? See, there is my card. I have a story to tell you which I would rather tell you there than here. It relates to the relatives of your mother, Mary Gooderich."

A sudden flush rose in the young man's cheek, and he looked vaguely at the card he had taken.

"I am at liberty, sir, and I will go with you," he said quietly, and Philip Heyward uttered a brief word of thanks. In Red Lion Street he hailed a passing hansom, and they drove out to Porchester Place. Both sat perfectly silent, the younger man full of vague, uncertain wonderings, the elder leaning back in his corner looking at the boyish, innocent face and figure, and thinking that in these womanish hands lay his destiny, that ere an hour was past these sweet lips might pronounce judgment and sentence upon him. Arrived at the house, Philip Heyward opened the hall door with his own key, and led the way to the library. A servant passing at the moment told her mistress a little later that the master and a strange young man had been in the house for nearly half-an-hour. Mrs. Heyward expressed no surprise, for though she knew her husband had intended making inquiries that day, she never for a moment connected the gentleman in the library with these inquiries. As the dinner-hour approached, however, she began to wonder what was the nature of the business which seemed to be so engrossing to her husband and the stranger downstairs. She was pacing up and down the room with a little nervousness of step when Philip entered the room. He was deadly pale, his face haggard and drawn, his eye gleaming with a strange fire. His manner and appearance betrayed the keenest mental excitement.

"Mildred, will you go down to the library? Mary Gooderich's son is there," was all he said.

She stood absolutely still, her eyes dilated with a sudden terror. Had the wronged man come to take her husband from her; to arraign him for the sin at the bar of an earthly court?

"I have told him the whole story; I hardly know how he has taken it," said Philip Heyward hurriedly. "He seems too much astonished to be able to realise fully the wrong I have done him. I wish you would go down at once."

"Come with me, then."

"No, I shall stay here. You need have no fear. He is a gentle, harmless boy. I believe he will be merciful to me, Mildred, in spite of the great wrong I have done him."

In a strange, mechanical fashion, Mildred Heyward walked out of the drawing-room, down the wide staircase, and without hesitating a moment entered the library. A figure standing at the table turned at her entrance, and looked at her with a keen and questioning glance. The graceful figure in its lustrous mourning garb, the sweet, sad face so deeply lined with care, the beautiful eyes bent with such wistful eagerness on his face, seemed to stir some strange chord in the young man's heart.

She moved swiftly to his side, and, to his bewilderment, knelt down, and folded pleading hands near to his on the table.

"I am Philip Heyward's wife, come to plead for my husband," she said, with a sob in her voice. "He has grievously sinned, but he has been grievously punished. I ask you to be merciful to him for my sake, and for the sake of the little child we buried only yesterday."

Walter Bernstein bent down, and with gentle hands, raised the drooping figure by his side.

"Rise, madam, why should you kneel to me?" he said, a little tremulously. "Then this strange and wonderful story is no dream, but a true reality; and I am indeed no longer a poor struggling youth, but the possessor of a great fortune!"

"Which by right ought to have been yours at the time of your uncle's death," supplemented Mildred Heyward, sadly, "but that my husband was tempted and fell."

"I have but one regret, Mrs. Heyward," said Walter Bernstein, dreamily—"that my angel-mother had not lived to see this day. What a joy to have surrounded her with every comfort, to atone in a measure for the many sad sufferings of her unselfish life; but, doubtless, as it is, it must be for the best."

Mildred Heyward looked at the fair face in wonder. There was not a shadow of reproach upon it, not a note of bitterness in the gentle voice. Verily, this man seemed to be moulded of different clay from his fellows.

"You have it in your hands, as you know, to expose and ruin my husband," she said, tremblingly. "We could neither wonder nor complain if you did so at once; but if you can find it in your heart to deal leniently with him, you will earn a woman's lifelong gratitude and love."

A sunny smile illuminated the fair, kind face.

"Dear Mrs. Heyward, who am I that I should judge or punish a fellow-creature? Should I, in a like temptation have been able to triumph? Believe me, your husband is safe so far as I am concerned; the story he has told to me shall never cross my lips again. Do I not know the acute sufferings of remorse he has borne? It is written on his face."

"May God for ever bless and reward you!" fell brokenly from the lips of Philip Heyward's wife; and the over-charged heart found relief in tears.

Chapter Nineteen

NO SHADOW

"BUT, Mildred, what on earth is the meaning of it? Has Philip encountered any serious losses in his business? I never heard of anything so extraordinary, so unlooked for! I am perfectly at sea. Do explain the matter to me, I entreat." Lady Vere sank breathlessly into a chair, and vigorously fanned herself with a dainty Japanese fan lying on the *bijou* table at her side. She was alone with her daughter in the latter's drawing-room, and had just been informed quietly that her son-in-law intended to remove from the house in Porchester Place to one much less pretentious, and that their establishment was to be very considerably reduced.

"Dear mamma, I can tell you nothing except that circumstances necessitate the change," answered Mildred quietly, though she seemed a little nervous under her mother's questioning. "It is no part of a wife's duty to divulge her husband's private concerns, is it, mother?"

"Nor is it part of a daughter's duty to deny her confidence to her mother," retorted Lady Vere, sharply. "I am afraid Philip must have been deceiving us all along."

"Hush, mamma!" said Mildred quickly. "Pray don't trouble yourself so about us. I shall be just as happy in a smaller house as I have been in this one; nay, happier," she added under her breath, with most passionate earnestness.

"Really, you are an absurd creature, Mildred; but you never had any proper pride. How do you suppose I am to explain matters to my friends?" asked Lady Vere, indignantly.

"Don't attempt it. Don't speak of us at all, mamma," said Mildred, lightly. "I assure you if you could be as indifferent to the world's opinion as I am, you would be much happier."

"I don't know that it is advisable to become careless of the world's opinion. We have a duty we owe to society, and which should prevent us giving people occasion to talk," said Lady Vere loftily, airing a favourite subject. "But it is of no use trying to improve your mind or imbue you with any proper feeling."

Mildred laughed, and walking over to the window looked out upon the budding trees in the gardens with eyes dim with intense thankfulness. It was the month of February now, three months since the baby died, three months, too, since that terrible revelation, which, after all, had brought truest peace and happiness to Mildred's heart. For now there was no shadow between her husband and herself; no inner door in his heart shut against her; they were indeed one in the highest and truest sense of the word. Philip Heyward was now a humble, gentle, child-like man, feebly groping in the upward way, thankful that the terrible burden he had borne so long had rolled away at last. Very sweet is the haven to the storm-tossed mariner, very sweet the cross to the weary soul when he has laid his burden down. Walter Bernstein came often to the house in Porchester Place, drawn there by the sweet magnet of Mildred Heyward's presence. And through love for her he was drawn to the husband who was so dear to her, and thus became a firm, warm friend of both.

"And Philip is at Linborough. Why didn't you go?" said Lady Vere presently.

"Because Philip wanted to go alone, mamma; he had some particular business with Jack, and it was not at all necessary that I should go," replied Mildred; but she did not say that his errand there was to tell his mother and brother the true reason for the change in their manner of life.

"He is really a fine young fellow, that Doctor Heyward," said Lady Vere, with condescending approval. "I shouldn't wonder to see him a Court physical yet. I met Sir Andrew Beauchamp at Mrs. Bentinck's dinner the other evening, and he spoke very highly of him. He had met him at a consultation at Linborough a few weeks since."

"Yes, I quite believe what you say. We are very fond and very proud of Doctor Heyward, mamma," said Mildred, with a little tender smile.

"And when is Philip coming home?"

"This afternoon. I was just looking out, thinking he might have come by the four o'clock train. Yes, there he is, and Jack, too," she exclaimed joyfully. "This is quite an unexpected pleasure. Excuse me one minute, mamma while I run down and greet him."

It was better that Lady Vere's cold eye should not be a witness to the deep emotion of that meeting. Philip Heyward stooped and fondly kissed his wife's fair face as he met her at the foot of the stairs; and the next moment Jack had her hands clasped in his, and his fine face was shining upon her sunnily as in the happy past.

"I had to come, Mildred, just to say thank God, and God bless you and Phil once more," he said, and the tears he felt on his hand told that Mildred knew and understood. "So the last days will be far, far better than the first—not the first time a little child's ministry on earth has been richly blessed."

She nodded, and a smile broke like sunshine through her tears. She led the way up to the drawing-room, and Lady Vere was very gracious in her demeanour to the young physician, though very stiff and constrained towards her son-in-law. It was not so much at the impending changes that the frivolous woman was annoyed as at the fact that she was not made aware of the circumstances which necessitated them. Tea was brought up presently, and just as Mildred seated herself behind the tray, a visitor was announced—Mr. Walter Bernstein. He was warmly greeted by Mr. and Mrs. Heyward, and Jack, forgetful of conventional rules, very fervently gripped his hand, and the eloquent look which accompanied the pressure assured the young man that Doctor Heyward was perfectly well aware of the circumstances which had led up to his being a frequent and welcome guest at Porchester Place. Jack was greatly taken with his frank, amiable, and unaffected manner, and saw ampled confirmation of his brother's warm praises of Walter Bernstein.

It was a pleasant tea-drinking. Bernstein, who had now ample time and means to follow the bent of his genius, talked chiefly of the pictures in a private gallery he had visited that morning; and Jack was quick to note how pleased he seemed to tell Mildred all about what he had seen, and with what admiring reverence his eyes followed her every movement. Evidently he had found some of the attributes of home in this pleasant drawing-room—a sweet experience for one without a home or kith and kin in the world.

While Doctor Heyward was courteously listening to Lady Vere's small talk, and Philip looking meditatively out of the window, Walter Bernstein approached the table where Mildred sat.

"Mrs. Heyward, is it true what I heard to-day, that you are to quit this house and move into a smaller one?" he asked in a low voice; "that your way of life is about to change in every way?"

"It is true, Walter," Mildred answered, with reddening cheeks.

"Is it because—because of, you know what?" he said hurriedly. "If I thought that in taking that money I had in any way hurt you I should hate myself."

"Hush, hush!" she whispered very low.

"Dear Mrs. Heyward, let me speak," he said with impetuous eagerness. "What is the use of all this money to me? I can never spend it. Why should you suffer while I have plenty?—you, who have been so good to me, who have made your house a home to me, the only one I have known since my mother died!"

Mildred lifted her eyes to his face, and, even in their gentleness, they were full of firmness.

"Walter, if you love us, never speak so again. What you say is impossible. Believe me, we do not the less feel your unselfish generosity because it will be impossible for us to accept it," she said, earnestly. "We shall not suffer. We shall not feel the sting of poverty, as you seem to think. Mr. Heyward's income from his business will be more than sufficient for our need and comfort. You cannot understand with what joy I shall exchange this fine house, where I have suffered so much, for a plainer abode which will be truly our own, and where we shall not be haunted by any spectre of self-reproach."

"I begin to understand," said the lad simply. "I did not think of that. Pray forgive me; I did not mean to hurt or vex you."

"Nay, do I not know that?" she said with a sunny smile. "And remember, Walter, that though our new home may be smaller, there will always be room in it for you. It will be as much your home—nay more, I trust, than this has ever been."

"Dear me! you two seem very intent. Is art the subject?" cried Lady Vere, a trifle impatiently. "Mr. Bernstein, you must positively come and talk to me, and tell me the subject of your new picture."

"I have no new picture, Lady Vere," said Walter, mildly; "you forget I am only a pupil yet."

"Well, do come and tell me about your studies, then," she said coquettishly, and made room on the ottoman beside her. Walter Bernstein was a great favourite of

Lady Vere's, though she had quite failed to get at his antecedents, or to fathom the mystery of his intimacy in her son-in-law's house. But as he was wealthy and distinguished, as well as artistic-looking, she was content to receive him very graciously. Doctor Heward, not sorry to be released from her ladyship's chatter, crossed to his sister-in-law's side.

"You will excuse me for a few hours, Mildred. I am going out to Finsbury Park," he said, as he set down his cup. "I shall be up probably about eight to remain over night, if you will keep me."

"Gladly; but Herbert is not at home," she said in a slightly surprised voice.

"No, but I promised before he went away to Germany to go and see the ladies sometimes, and——"

"And what?"

"I was about to say something which would perhaps be better left unsaid," he said, meaningly. But she was quick to understand.

"The fulfilment of your promise is not irksome to you, Jack?" she said, with a very tender smile.

"How quick you are to read between the lines," he said, with an answering smile. "When the time comes, *you* will wish me God-speed, Mildred?"

"Yes, I think her worthy even to fill that vacant place, Jack," Mildred answered softly. "She is more like Edith than any human being I have ever met."

"That drew me to her first; but it will not be yet awhile," Jack answered, and there was no more said; but it seemed to the happy heart of Mildred Heyward that every cloud was rolling away from the troubled sky, that her cup was filling fast to the very brim. Verily the Lord had put a new song in her mouth, whose every note was thanksgiving and heartfelt praise.

In the twilight that night, after all the guests had gone, and before Jack had returned, Philip Heyward and his wife had a few quiet moments alone together in the dusky drawing-room. "I went to see those houses to-day, Milly," he said. "The rents are uniform, seventy-five pounds; and the accommodation, though it seemed a little limited to me, is just such as you spoke of. There are two reception rooms, a small study, and five bed-rooms."

"That will do very nicely, dear; and if we can find a tenant to take the furniture here at a valuation, it will be better, and then we can buy suitable things for our smaller domain. Why, Philip, do not look so sad! Am I not positively glorying in the prospect of the change?"

"Yes, but *I* am not. When I think of you in such a house, my darling, with two domestics to assist you in its management, I feel rather peculiar, I tell you," he said, smiling, in spite of himself, for it was impossible to resist the dancing eyes uplifted to his face.

"Then you are a very ungrateful, unthankful sort of person, Philip, and you don't deserve so good a wife," she said, but in a moment her bantering mood changed, and she laid her head upon his arm, and continued in earnest tones: "Oh, my dearest, I cannot tell you how happy, how *thankful* I am! I really feel that I could bear no more happiness just at present, my heart is so full. This is the first time in my life that I have felt absolutely free from care."

"My darling, I will do what one man can to shield you from every care henceforth," he said, drawing her very close to him. "When I think of all you have been and are to me, my wife, it almost unmans me. God knows that in my heart of hearts I am not ungrateful for His infinite mercy to me. May He help me to show it by my actions in the future."

"We will work together for Him, dear. We will give part of our substance for His case year by year to mark our gratitude," said Mildred, softly. "Please God, we will not henceforth live only for each other, but for that higher and more perfect life which will be ours when our work on earth is done."

"You will help me, Mildred, even as you have done so infinitely in the past," he said, with that humbleness of manner and tone which always broke her down. "Without you I am nothing; with you I feel as if I could live a life which will not be quite unworthy in its aims, nor quite fruitless in its influences and results."

"God will help us both if we only ask Him, dear; He has wonderfully helped us hitherto," she said, with bright, grave earnestness. "I expect great things from you, my husband, and I will tell you something which ought, nay must, chase away that gravity from your face. It is that never were you so unspeakably dear to me as now, and that there is no happier wife than yours in all England. There, I see you smile, and that is Jack's ring at the bell. Let us go down."

*   *   *

There are other children now in Philip Heyward's

happy home, but the little Eric is not, and never will be, forgotten. The green enclosure in the churchyard at Hadley, where he sleeps besides his grandfather, is never without its wreath and freshly-culled flowers at the base of the cross, which records that here sleeps:

"JOHN ERIC,
Eldest Child of Philip and Mildred
Heyward, of London."

Lower down, these words are inscribed in golden Letters:

"Of such is the Kingdom of Heaven."

And the little ones, who have come sometimes with their father and mother to visit. "Aunt Cecil" at Hadley Manor, weave dainty daisy chains with grave lips and loving fingers for the grave of the little brother whom "having not seen, they love."

A successful man in business life is Philip Heyward, and his name is held in high honour among his fellow-men. His word is as good as his bond, and those who deal with him in business would trust him with untold gold. He is even called fastidious and crotchety in his rigid integrity, extreme in his ideas of justice and honour. They do not know, of course, of his unhappy past, they cannot understand that he cannot afford to be otherwise than sternly scrupulous now. The few who are admitted into the precincts of that blessed home, go away wondering why it is different from other houses, why the inmates seem to breathe a purer, sweeter air, why the place in its unutterable peace should almost savour of heaven. It is because the blessing of God, which maketh rich and addeth no sorrow, abides continually upon that household—because its inmates walk in love together in the narrow way of life, and so are laying up for themselves treasures in heaven.

Dr. Heyward practises now in the West End of London. Although he is not yet a Court physician, he numbers among his patients many distinguished personages, by whom he is as much beloved for himself as he is honoured for his great professional skill. He is no longer alone. The time came when he went down to Finsbury Park on a special errand, and not in vain. And, though the memory of his first love can never be forgotten, it is no divided love he has given to his wife; she knows that, and her gentle heart is not disturbed in any way by the memory of her who sleeps within sight of the sounding sea, upon the green and lovely shores of Sussex. Nor are those dwelling still at Kingsmead Manor, and who so cherish the dear memory of Edith Lancaster, jealous of her who has filled her place. Nay, as became them, they were glad with and for him; and if, of the three sprite who make merry the house in Queen's Gate, the little Edith should be the most fondly welcome at Kingsmead, the gentle mother can smile tenderly at it, and think it only natural.

Lady Vere still flutters airily through life, indefatigable in her devotion to society, and refusing to believe that she is growing old. When she visits her daughter in her own home, she feels vaguely that there is something lacking in her life, but pathetically attributes it to her widowed and childless state. Mildred prays for her mother and hopes, knowing that with God all things are possible. The other two mothers, Mrs. Heyward and Mrs. St. John, being left alone, make their home together, and are happy, because they are kindred spirits, and the monotony of their life is pleasantly varied by frequent visits to their children in their various homes. Herbert is an army surgeon, at present serving with the forces in Egypt. He has his father's dauntless courage, and what is better, his high and honourable Christian character. Walter Bernstein, after years of patient study, is coming very near the realisation of his life's dream, and is spoken of in artistic circles as the most promising of all the later students of art. Needless to say, he is still "at home" beneath Philip Heyward's roof-tree. He says it is Mrs. Heyward's influence that has made him what he is. And so, having come thus far with my friends upon their way, I say farewell.

THE END